Author Photo [TK]

Nelly Reifler
ELECT H. MOUSE STATE JUDGE

Nelly Reifler is the author of *See Through*, a collection of short stories. Her work has appeared in a range of publications, including *McSweeney's*, *Bomb*, *Black Book*, *Nerve*, *Lucky Peach*, and *jubilat*. She is on the editorial staff at *Post Road* and teaches at Sarah Lawrence and Pratt Institute.

Also by Nelly Reifler

See Through

ELECT
H. MOUSE
STATE JUDGE

ELECT
H. MOUSE
STATE JUDGE

Nelly Reifler

ff

FABER AND FABER, INC.
AN AFFILIATE OF FARRAR, STRAUS AND GIROUX
NEW YORK

Faber and Faber, Inc.
An affiliate of Farrar, Straus and Giroux
18 West 18th Street, New York 10011

Library of Congress Cataloging-in-Publication Data
Reifler, Nelly.
    Elect H. Mouse State Judge / Nelly Reifler. — 1st ed.
        p.   cm.
    ISBN 978-0-86547-765-0 (pbk. : alk. paper)
    1. Kidnapping—Fiction.   2. Private investigators—Fiction.
I. Title.

PS3618.E555E44 2013
813'.6—dc23   2012034572

Designed by Jonathan D. Lippincott

www.fsgbooks.com
www.twitter.com/fsgbooks • www.facebook.com/fsgbooks

1   3   5   7   9   10   8   6   4   2

Acknowledgments (TK)

For Jonathan Dixon

ELECT
H. MOUSE
STATE JUDGE

ONE

1

H. Mouse was running for State Judge. He had diligently worked his way up the ranks from apprentice to secretary to uniformed guard to courtroom stenographer to lawyer to attorney to village councillor. And now the day had come for him to place the ballot box out on his porch and invite the citizens to vote for him. He'd taken a red box, emptied of its succulent raisins, and covered it in white paper. He'd cut a slot in the top, wide enough to easily slip in a folded ballot, but not so wide that ballots could be as easily slipped out. He'd weighted it down with gravel from his circular driveway so that the brisk autumn breeze would not pick it up and blow it away. And on the front he wrote in large print letters, ELECT H. MOUSE STATE JUDGE.

He hefted it off the mudroom floor and balanced it on his plump belly. Then he waddled outside to his porch. It certainly was a fine day, thought H. Mouse. Up and down his street sat handsome, symmetrical houses, all with up-stairs and downstairs, with shutters and porches. All had real outlets with real electricity into which you could plug real lamps that really lit up. Each had a chiffonier that opened and closed, containing wineglasses, plates, and a roast turkey or a shiny ham decorated with brown criss-crosses. The houses had rugs and beds. Some had a coat rack, an umbrella, a framed Impressionist print; others a refrigerator, towels, a cradle. H. Mouse felt enriched thinking of the things in his neighbors' houses and his own. Times were good, he thought, neighbors were happy and prosperous and everybody was organized and clean and lived with the satisfaction of knowing true order. It would be a perfect moment for him to ascend to his newest role in his career as a public servant. It was the right time for his message.

He pulled up one of his real wood rocking chairs and awaited the voters' visits.

2

The Sunshine Family huddled in their green plastic van. They had round eyes, smooth chests, and short legs.

Mother Sunshine said, "It is time."

Father Sunshine said, "Now is the moment as has been ordained by destiny."

Mother Sunshine handed Father Sunshine the long-distance binoculars. Girl Sunshine and Boy Sunshine hopped up and down. The hinges of their knees and ankles squeaked. In unison they chanted, "Enlarge the family, enlarge the race. Widen the circle, tighten the brace."

"Hush, children. Father is plotting our next move." Mother Sunshine smoothed her calico apron down with her curved fingers. The children dropped to the floor, sounding twin thuds with their hard behinds.

It had been a long encampment here in the forest on the edge of town. When you are on a mission for something greater than yourself, you are willing to wait for the opportunity to take action. The van was parked in a circle of trees a quarter mile off the old dirt fire trail. For many moons Mother Sunshine had been cooking the family's meals of rice gruel and poached varmints over an open fire. The children had been memorizing the words of the Book of Doctrines, and repeating its hieratical ordinations to each other. And Father Sunshine had been calculating, communicating in the Old Language, through whispers, with the Power, waiting for a sign.

"He has moved to the porch," said Father Sunshine, adjusting the focus on the binoculars. "He has carried the ballot box out there with him. I see he has pulled up a real wood rocking chair. Now he is sitting down."

"And the others?" asked Mother Sunshine.

"Readying themselves for their new life, although they are not yet conscious of this truth."

3

Susie Mouse handed Margo Mouse a rag doll. "Pretend you're the teacher now," said Susie. "I'll be the bad student who gets punished, and this is the principal. Send me to the principal's office."

Margo said nothing.

"Margo!"

Margo turned her head slowly. "What?"

"Stop staring out the window. Be the teacher."

Margo's white eyelet dress was wrinkled and her barrette was dangling off her ear. She turned her head back toward the window.

"You're hopeless," said Susie. "You're a loser."

"There's something out there," said Margo.

"There is not. I've told you already. It's the same stupid elm and the same dumb old swing set, and the shed and the fence. That's what's out there."

"Something's watching." Margo pointed. Susie followed with her eyes and squinted. The attic playroom had a view of the village, with its shops and roundabout and benches. Beyond that, the sisters could see the sparse edge of town, where the few houses were surrounded by acres of fields, and where the service road was dotted with the occasional gas station, low strip mall, or diner. The dark, wild forest rose up in the distance. The trees formed a mass that looked solid, impenetrable. It was hard to believe that there was earth under those trees, that there were living creatures in the fortress of those hills.

"How could anything be watching from that far away?" said Susie. "You're just all stressed out because it's Election Day. You worry about Dad too much."

"I don't know." Margo shook her head. "It's not about the election. I'm afraid."

"Don't be ridiculous."

But Margo noticed that Susie's voice sounded a little less shrill, and that the words came out a little more slowly.

"Forget it," said Margo. "What were we playing?"

4

"Wait here," said Father Sunshine, making the sign of the Dodecahedron over each of his children's heads. Girl Sunshine and Boy Sunshine sat on their piece of foam rubber in the corner. Their legs jutted out in front of them. They stared straight ahead.

"It is windy today," said Mother Sunshine. The tin cans dangling from a clothesline, set up to repel bears, clanked against each other tunelessly.

"If the Power fells me with an enloosened branch, so it is to be," said Father Sunshine. "Do not mourn for me; I will have joined the Twelve Hundred Celestial Angel-demons. If the Power fells me, you must carry on the Project."

"I shall," said Mother Sunshine.

Father Sunshine bent his hip hinges, pulled on some pants, slung his backpack over his shoulders, and strapped his pistol into his belt.

5

H. Mouse thought about the things he would do as State Judge. He would decide who gets what. And whether this one or that one goes to jail or goes free. He'd talk to the citizens about fines and rewards. He'd pick juries and teach them all about the law. He couldn't remember a time in his life when doing good and furthering the cause of fairness were not the twin beating hearts of his being. Rocking on his porch, he thought of the word *parity*, and about how he believed that each of us is basically good, equally so—no matter how some may stray because of their stressful circumstances. If everybody could be given the proper tools for moral strength and ethical decision-making, theft would end. And abuse. And dishonesty.

After all, he told himself, when pushed into a corner or backed to the edge of a precipice, the best of us might find ourselves doing things of which we never imagined we were capable.

A picture flickered through his mind like a bat, but he shooed it away. His stomach squeezed and he suddenly tasted acid in his mouth. Was he hungry? He patted his belly and looked at the sky. It was close to noon, and he was indeed feeling rather munchy. He could picture the tray of muffins baked by his daughter Margo that morning, sitting out on the counter, where she had set them to cool.

But what was this coming down the street? Why, it was Fernanda Gekko, with a folded piece of paper. She seemed to be, as usual, dressed to the nines, with a flowing skirt, long gloves, satin bonnet, and alligator purse. H. Mouse pushed himself up from the real wood rocking chair and brushed his vest in case of stray dandruff. He buttoned the vest button that always popped open when he sat. He waved at Fernanda as she approached his porch.

"Ms. Gekko, how delightful to see you."

"H.," she said, daintily gathering the cloth of her skirt to ascend the porch steps. Lace-up boots of aubergine leather peeked from her petticoat. "It's my pleasure to cast a ballot in your ballot box today."

"I cannot thank you enough for your support." He gave a slight bow.

"You're the candidate for me." Her eyes seemed to grow a little wetter as she added, "You're one of the few good ones out there, H."

He smiled at her. He didn't know what had happened in her past, but he wanted to reassure her. "Ms. Gekko, we are all good, each and every one of us. Some are just weak, but none are hopeless."

"That's an extremely charitable point of view," she said. "Another reason I'm doing this." And with that, she dropped the folded paper through the slot of H. Mouse's box.

"Well, thank you again. Thanks for coming by."

Fernanda Gekko patted his sleeve and sighed as she turned and descended the steps. He watched her walk away, down the street toward the center of the village. There was nothing wrong with looking.

6

As their father chatted on the porch, Susie and Margo were being dragged away from their home in a sack. Father Sunshine had been conversing with the Power for many rotations of the earth, offering his loyalty. In exchange, the Power had bestowed upon Father Sunshine the lessons needed to focus his Pyramidal Tract, the section of the brain that was implanted by the Ancients in order to channel their energy from generation to generation. This energy endowed Father Sunshine with the Strength of the Dozen. Even though his captives wriggled a little in the bag, they were silent (he had gagged them with wadded cloth and tape) and relatively still (he had trussed them with Manila rope).

Without the sisters' knowledge, the Power had guided them out of their high playroom and into the kitchen, where they had been standing when Father Sunshine reached the house. He had peeked through the window: they were leaning against the counter, eating some kind of baked good and laughing. He forgave them for taking pleasure in the corporeal decadence of sugar and leavening. They did not know yet, that was all. He would have to grab them both at once.

He had opened the screen door, pistol in his hand.

The littler one saw him first. She opened her mouth, gasping, showing him its white, wet contents.

He whispered to them, "Do not make a sound, or the Power will shoot this gun and kill your bodies. You are lucky. You are part of the Universal Plan. You have been picked for the Ascendant Widening of the Circle." He jabbed the gun in the air, pointing it alternately at the stomach of one and then the other. "The Power will not harm your bodies if you stand still now." They had stood still. That was when he had pulled the tape, cloth, and rope from his belt.

Did he question the Power for even a second? Did he ask why the Power had sent him these two, with their beady black eyes and plump little vessel bodies that only reached as high as his hip hinges? Of course he did not.

Now he reached the fence at the rear of the adjacent property. He had clipped it a month ago, and the loosened portion toppled easily. Turning left from there it was a straight shot through one more yard, then up an alley behind the water-treatment station to the mouth of the winding forest road. He knew he would have to carry them, not just tow them, once he hit pavement. At the base of the forest road he would pick up the old all-terrain vehicle he had hidden behind a shed, stuff the sisters in the sidecar, and ride to the fire trail. There was a second unused shed there, where he could once again stow the vehicle. Mother, Boy, and Girl Sunshine would be waiting at the fire trail. He figured that at that point, they wouldn't need the sack anymore. Everyone could walk back to the van together.

7

Susie and Margo both went utterly limp inside the sack. It was dark, and the uneven ground moving under their bodies bumped and bruised them. Susie concentrated on breathing; she felt as if she might forget to breathe and then die. Margo was shocked by how real it all felt, how it was happening now, at this very moment—but on the other hand, she wasn't surprised at all. She had known something was coming. She had known it was going to get them.

Each sister kept her body close to the other, to the extent that it was possible.

8

Where were they?

H. Mouse stumbled on a rag doll that lay, arms and legs splayed haphazardly, directly on the threshold between the kitchen and the mudroom.

He called their names.

Nothing. This wasn't like his daughters. Gripping the banister, he waddled up the stairs to their bedroom. Neatly made twin captain's beds, more dolls, the grasshopper in its cage, running round and round on its grasshopper wheel. At the base of the attic steps he called again: "Susie! Margo!"

Maybe they were playing a game, he thought. They were good and sweet. They weren't prone to practical jokes. But it was true that Susie was reaching the age where she'd begun to form an identity outside the family unit; could she have roped Margo into some harebrained scheme to worry H. sick? He pulled himself up the attic steps. He imagined his daughters hiding in a corner under the eaves, whispering to each other in that secret language of theirs—Obby, they called it. He imagined them covering their mouths and trying to stay quiet as they heard him approaching. He imagined them jumping out and shouting, "Boo!" at him and then collapsing in giggles. But the attic was dim and empty. He stepped over another doll that was sitting at a shoe-box desk. There was a low shelf holding picture books pressed under the slanted ceiling, and behind it a triangular cavity. He grunted a little as he heaved the shelf out from its spot. Nothing back there but shadows.

His heart pounded. Maybe they'd gone over to visit one of the neighbors. But as he had the thought, he understood that he'd only had it because it's one of the things you're supposed to think when your children suddenly go missing. Even so, he made his way back down to the kitchen, where he picked up the receiver of the wall phone.

"Operator."

"Give me Eldridge 3-7717," said H. Mouse.

After a couple of rings Sally Gerbil picked up. "Hello?" came her creaky voice.

"Sally, it's H."

"Oh, yes, H. Thank you for the call. I nearly forgot it was Election Day. I'll toddle over to cast my ballot after tea and crumpets."

Election Day! H. stretched the phone cord as far as it would go and peered out the dining-room windows at the porch. The ballot box was still there.

"Sally, you haven't seen Margo and Susie today, have you?"

"The little ones? Nope. Haven't seen 'em."

Next he called Binne Volesdöttir, on the other side, who said in her thick accent that she hadn't seen them either. Nor had Pinkney Plastic-Hat across the street.

He found himself slouched on the kitchen floor, head hanging, legs bunched up against his chest. From this vantage point, the crumbs and dried, moldy vegetable scraps around the edge of the linoleum looked like miniature, multicolor snowdrifts. An ant climbed one of the drifts and selected a morsel, wiggling its antennae. H. had always thought he had a clean kitchen; he hadn't realized it housed a tiny world of dirt and decay. When he raised his eyes a little bit, though, he noticed that some of the crumbs were in the middle of the floor, and they seemed to have fallen in a line—all the way to the back door off the mudroom. He crawled over to one cluster of crumbs, picked some, and sniffed them. They were soft and fresh: bits of Margo's blueberry muffins—the mostly full tray of which still sat on the counter.

He took a deep breath. It was sinking in. He had no idea where his daughters were. He reached for the edge of the counter and pulled himself back up to standing. He grew dizzy for a moment while the blood rushed out of his head. He took a couple of deep breaths, then returned to the phone to ring the direct number for Bub Flytrap, the police commissioner. H. had known Bub ever since they'd been apprentices together, double-dating and playing pickup mumblety-peg in the park. Oh, those were the days!

"Operator."

"Give me——" H. started. Then he stopped, his voice catching in his throat. "Never mind."

H. hung up the phone and sank back down to the kitchen floor.

9

Margo and Susie found themselves standing in a scrubby clearing in the woods. They were sore all over. They'd been piled, still inside the sack, on some vibrating machine, noisy and smelly.

Now they were unbound. Their limbs were weak from the trauma, and the ropes had cut off their circulation, leaving their extremities numb. Margo looked down at one of her legs and saw that it was badly scraped and bleeding. She tried to bend down to brush the dirt out of her wound, but she was too unsteady on her feet and fell over. Their captor took a few stiff steps toward her and offered his hard, shiny hand to help her up.

"The others will be here soon," he said.

Susie started to cry again, drooling around the wad of cloth in her mouth. Margo, with great effort, reached over and touched her sister. Susie always cried first, and often the moments when Susie cried—scary movies, thunderstorms—were the same moments that Margo felt like she was separating from her body and hovering at a slight distance, watching.

A minute later, three figures came clomping toward them over the brush. They moved choppily, with legs that stuck out in front of them and hinged arms that clicked back and forth. One had yellow hair and a long dress with an apron. The other two, who were smaller, had darker hair and wore green outfits with silver emblems on them. Their skin was uniformly pink and shiny. Their eyes were blue spheres with big black pupils.

They stopped before Margo and Susie. The one in the dress bent at her hips and clicked her arms out, pulling first Margo, then Susie, close. Margo smelled smoke and mildew and plastic.

"Welcome, our dear new Spirit Carriers. I am Mother Sunshine. I know this is all very surprising to you now, but soon you will begin receiving the Ancient Teachings as are laid out in the Book of Doctrines. You are extremely special. You have been chosen to help fulfill the prophesies."

The male captor spoke. "Whatever you think your names are, they are no longer of use to you. From now on you are Vessel Alpha and Vessel Omega."

The smaller figures stepped forward now. One said, "I am Boy Sunshine."

The other said, "I am Girl Sunshine.

In unison they chanted, "Welcome, sisters. Join us in the Dodecahedron."

Margo and Susie noticed then that the smaller figures had stepped into the middle of a circle—well, not exactly a circle—delineated on the ground by small rocks that glittered with mica. The one who called herself Mother Sunshine gave Margo and Susie little pushes, and they stumbled into the space. Mother Sunshine smiled ecstatically. Father Sunshine marched over and stuck his arm into the glittering space. Margo felt his cold hand hanging over her head. She moved her eyes and saw that Susie was trembling. Father Sunshine muttered something Margo couldn't understand.

And then Margo and Susie were led, slowly and gently, along the path into the depths of the woods.

10

It was late afternoon now. A steady stream of voters had been casting their ballots for hours. H. Mouse felt as if he were performing a dreadful pantomime, waving, greeting them, thanking them, giving the little bow that was one of his trademark gestures.

There was still no sign of Margo and Susie. But H. had realized it with utter clarity in that moment at the telephone: he couldn't go to the town police for help. Not on—or anytime near—Election Day. He knew better than anyone how local justice worked: even if he were the one to report his daughters missing, the authorities would be required to rule him out as a suspect. Standard procedure—in fact, one of H.'s own cases back when he was an attorney (*Citizens v. Fawn Doe*) had set the precedent for it. If he made a fuss and asked for special treatment, it would undercut his campaign's primary message of fairness and equal treatment for all. But if he let them begin digging around in his past—well, no, he just couldn't let that happen. No more than he could have them dig around in his present. He'd come all this way without anybody poking their snouts where he didn't want their snouts.

Now he sat in the darkened den, holding a strong cordial. He reassured himself. Again. Whatever may or may not have happened behind the scenes had nothing to do with his ability to serve in public office. He was a good servant of the citizens; their lives were his charge, and he took his duties as seriously as a priest.

He sighed and put down his empty glass. Standing, he buttoned his vest and pulled his car key out of his pocket.

There was only one place he could go for help.

Barbie and Ken were fucking. They were fucking and screwing and doing it. They did it like bunnies and dogs and horses. Poolside, they humped, slamming against each other, grinding, wedging their legs into each other's crotches. Skipper watched on in her plaid jumper, bored.

"Unh, unh, unh," said Ken.

"Ah, ah, ah," said Barbie.

Skipper bent her leg daintily at the knee. "Don't you guys have a job to do or something?"

The truth was, they had just finished a job, and that was what made them so horny. They always got like this after they were paid.

Barbie popped off her head, and Ken stuck his hand inside the cavity where her neck ball had been.

"Oooh, yeah," said Barbie.

"Oh, baby, it feels so good to be inside you," said Ken. "Do you like this? When I move it like this?"

"Yes," she said. "Oh, yes, I do."

Ken grasped Barbie's head and lifted his right leg up. He stuck his foot inside her head. Barbie moaned. The whole orange inflatable deck shook as Ken rocked in and out.

Skipper took out a pink nail file and ran it along her fingertips. She looked out at the view. From where she sat on a clear blow-up chair, she could see the whole valley: the cute little town below, with its uniform houses where regular folk lived, its roundabout, its market center, the murky mountains beyond. The sun was setting behind the mountains. Here in the southern hills it was always warm and dry, and that was nice, but every so often she wished to know what it was like in the cool valley or up on the foggy mountains. Lazily, she directed her gaze back across the deck.

Ken, his foot still inside Barbie's head, removed his own head and passed it to Barbie. Barbie gripped it and rubbed the brown hair across her chestbumps in circular motions.

"Now." Ken's mouth spoke. "C'mon, baby. Give it to me now."

Barbie lifted Ken's head, and lowered it—teasingly slow—onto her own neckball. She rolled his head around on the pink orb that topped her long, slender neck. Ken withdrew his foot and put Barbie's head on his neckball. Then they slammed their bodies together once again.

"Unh, unh, unh," said Ken.

"Ah, ah, ah," said Barbie.

The wavelike motions were starting to get to Skipper. She stood up and made her way delicately across the deck, down the gleaming white stone walkway, to the threshold of the pink townhouse. Her pink twirling baton was leaning against the door. She picked it up and twirled it a couple of times. Inside, she rode the elevator to her room on the second floor.

12

How he hated to do it. H. Mouse got out of his brown sedan at a turnaround on Floralinda Drive, a good distance from his destination. God forbid anyone see his car parked at the place itself. It was hot over here, even in the evening; succulents lined the byway, and sandy soil drifted onto the edges of Floralinda Drive's shiny tar surface.

He'd made this trip twice before: the first time was after he'd stupidly agreed to join a poker game, thinking it would be a nice way of connecting with the community; he'd wound up with some debt he needed to tuck away. The second time, well, that was worse. He'd let his urges get away with him, and someone needed to be encouraged, discretely, firmly, to leave town.

He trudged along the side of the road by the light of the occasional zinc streetlamp, stepping on ice plants and tiny aloes. Sweat poured down his face, and he mopped it off with a real cloth handkerchief. His tummy churned and he tried his best to push away the old images that fluttered around the eaves of his mind on bats' wings. He had forgotten lunch. He felt faint.

He paused at the bottom of the long, curving driveway and gazed up the hill. Palm trees arched over it, and parrots darted among their fronds, backlit by the sapphire late-dusk sky. He took off his vest, rolled up his sleeves, and unbuttoned the top two buttons of his shirt. Even in his state of panic and anxiety, H. couldn't help but notice the smells of desert herbs—rosemary and sage—floating in the gentle breeze.

The townhouse rose, magnificent, sparkling, on the hill. As H. approached, the pool came into view, and he could see that it was wobbling furiously.

He knew what to expect, and braced himself. He crossed the lawn, avoiding the sprinklers, and climbed the steps. The pool was illuminated by floodlights.

There they were, coupling as usual. Their long, lean, peach-colored bodies were contorting in jerky, synchronized motions. They moaned and gasped and grunted.

He sat down in one of the blow-up chairs and watched, oddly calmed by the sight of their calisthenics. There was a half-full glass of iced tea in the chair's cup holder; he drank it. It was sweet and slightly astringent.

When Barbie and Ken finally finished, and he saw that they had their own heads back on their neckballs, he cleared his throat.

Barbie spoke first: "Why, H. Mouse! What a surprise to see you here tonight."

"Yeah," said Ken, sitting in the other chair and pulling Barbie down onto his lap so she covered his groin-lump. "Isn't it Election Day?"

"Please," said H. "I'm really having an emergency here. I can't even express to you how dire this situation is. They're my life, my whole life . . ." He had told himself he wouldn't break down, but here he was, blubbering right in front of these, these . . . sleazy operators.

Barbie lit a cigarette and leaned in toward H. She stroked his sleeve with her free hand. "Hey now," she said in her twinkling voice. "Hey."

"H.," said Ken, taking a drag from Barbie's cigarette and then sticking it back between her pink lips, "My friend, H. We're here to help. We're at your service. What can we do you for?"

"It's Margo and Susie," murmured H., wiping his nose on his sweat-soaked sleeve. "My daughters. They're gone. One minute they were home, the next minute they were nowhere." He sobbed again. "Margo made blueberry muffins this morning." And as he said it, he felt a kind of vertigo. Had it really just been this morning that he'd passed by the kitchen doorway and seen his daughter standing on the little real wooden stool and measuring some flour out into a real sifter with parts that really move? "Just this morning . . . ," he repeated.

"Wait a minute," said Barbie. "What do you mean *they're gone.*"

"They disappeared. I think they were taken out the back door." H. took a deep breath. *Collect yourself,* he thought. "Okay, it's probably nothing. I'm probably over-reacting. I called around to the neighbors. No one saw anything. I didn't want to go further than that because, yes, it's Election Day. You know what that means, I presume?"

"Sure, sure," said Ken. "We get your drift. You're an upstanding citizen, a good leader. Scrutiny doesn't play well, even if you're the victim. And what if it's a false alarm? Why make a fuss?"

"And besides," said Barbie—did H. detect a slight twist in her tone?—"scrutiny of one kind can bring scrutiny of another. You wouldn't want that."

H. didn't have to be reminded that Barbie and Ken could ruin him. "No," he said evenly. "I wouldn't want that."

"What I think you're getting at," said Ken, "is that you need our help finding the kiddos. Am I right?"

"Yes," said H.

Barbie leaned forward. "Okay, let's assume they've been taken. Was there a ransom note?"

H. shook his head.

"And . . ." Barbie let a puff of cigarette smoke curl slowly from between her lips. "Do you think there's any chance this is an act of revenge?"

"Revenge?" H. tried to look shocked. Barbie tilted her head and fixed him with a cool, steady gaze. H. sighed. "Oh. No. I mean, I don't think so." A pulse of dizziness overtook him, and he flopped back on the inflatable plastic, eyes squeezed shut.

"Oh, H.," said Barbie, soft once again. He opened his eyes. She rose off Ken's lap. Then she cupped H.'s sweaty face in her elegant fingers. "Don't worry. We'll do everything we can to reunite you with your precious ones."

"For a price," said H.

"For a price," said Barbie.

TWO

13

If you know how to do it, you do it. Father Sunshine knew how to do it. How did he know? The Power told him. Often the Power whispered in his ears; sometimes the Power thundered in the wind. The prophesies alluded to the methods.

First, you must detoxify the Spirit Carriers from their addiction to food. You allow them one jar of water each hour while they are going through withdrawal. This ensures that they expel the tainted energy of indulgent consumption through their urine. Next, you teach them to Rest their bodies. To chant. To read the symbols of the hieratic ordinations. To absorb the jewels of the Dodecahedron.

Nourishment is useful in this training. Once the Sprit Carriers have been detoxified, they accept quite willingly the pure, unvoluptuous calories of rice gruel and woodland creatures. One can extend the promise of such a meal as a way to assure the inexperienced Spirit Carriers that they can trust you. When you bless the food and feed them, you are passing the Power into their vessel bodies.

If they refuse to learn, you know they are not ready to be fed, and you must tell them so. Soon, after some meditation, they will come around. After all, the Sprit Carriers have been chosen by the prophecies. It is just a matter of showing them that they must accept their wonderful destinies.

If they are tired, show them the way to Rest: lying on their backs, bellies to the sky, so the Power may enter and leave through their navels. Inhalations for four counts, Exhalations for eight. At first, they will only be ready for fifteen minutes of Rest at a time. They will not want to rise after fifteen minutes, but remind them they must because of the remnants of corruption that still live in their cells. Explain that they will be capable of longer Resting later, when they have let go of their old masks and false attachments. Sooner or later, they will understand their true purpose on the planet Earth. Their Pyramidal Tracts will vibrate in perfect harmony with their vessel bodies. They will experience the blissful satisfaction of fulfilling their ordained truths.

14

Somebody else was always with them; Mother Sunshine sat by them during their periods of rest and softly jostled them every fifteen minutes. Or Father Sunshine would instruct them to kneel, to bend, to press their foreheads to the floor. Boy or Girl Sunshine would bring them their water. "Drink," they would say. "It is for purification. Soon you will be emptied of toxicity and you may eat." Margo and Susie could only exchange glances. Neither had any idea what the other was thinking or feeling. Each one could only guess based on the expression she saw on her sister's face.

Susie, Vessel Alpha, was hungry. She was very hungry and tired, and she wanted to be hugged and told that everything was going to be okay. Time was funny. Had they been here a day? Days? She had no idea. Daylight and darkness ran together. Her stomach was growling, and she had a sour taste in her mouth that the cold mountain spring water fed to her by the Sunshine young could not wash away.

Kneeling next to Margo—Vessel Omega—before Father Sunshine on the chartreuse carpeting, Susie wondered if her sister was also so hungry and also had the sour taste. Margo appeared to be concentrating on Father Sunshine's words, looking up at him as he intoned a story about the Power and the creation of the invisible hieroglyphs. When you reach your full potential, Father Sunshine said, you are able not just to see but to read these ancient and sacred characters. Susie wondered if Margo hoped she would be able to see the hieroglyphs someday. Margo glanced over at Susie, and Susie thought she looked stern. Susie told herself to pay closer attention to Father Sunshine. If she was ever going to eat again, she had to reach some level of purity.

A little later, Susie and Margo sat on the floor across from Boy and Girl Sunshine.

"Are Father and Mother Sunshine your parents?" asked Susie.

"They are the lifewells of our vessel bodies," said Boy. "Father is our Teacher. He is your Teacher, too. Mother is our Shepherdess. She is your Shepherdess, too."

"Come, Vessel Omega," said Girl. "I will show you our water spigot."

"Why just *Omega*," Susie whined. She hadn't meant to, but her voice came out ugly and complaining.

"Because the Power has ordained it," said Girl. She stood and reached out her hand to Margo, pulling her to her feet.

"I will go help Father with the lookout," said Boy.

"I'll come, too," said Susie.

"No, Vessel Alpha. You must remain in the van," said Girl, leading Margo through the orange beaded curtains and out the back door. Boy left, too, grabbing a walking stick on his way out.

Susie sighed. She felt lonely and left out. Nobody loved her. Nobody understood her. She burped and squeezed her aching, empty belly. She began to cry.

Out of nowhere, Mother Sunshine appeared. She walked over to Susie and lowered herself onto the floor. She put her arms around Susie and pulled her close. Susie wept into Mother Sunshine's neck.

"It's all going to be alright," said Mother Sunshine. "This is the most difficult phase, but it will get better. It will be better than you can possibly imagine right now, little Vessel Alpha."

Susie looked up into Mother's eyes. "Really?" she said.

Mother smiled at her. "Yes. Now, come with me. I have something for you."

Susie followed Mother down the length of the van and into the kitchen nook behind the bucket seats. Something smelled like food. Susie's mouth began to water. Mother patted the bench that was attached to the small fold-down table. Susie sat down, and Mother placed a shallow plastic bowl in front of her. It contained a lump of something gray and mushy.

"The Power has told Father that you are ready to consume food," said Mother.

"Me?" said Susie. "Me and not Margo?"

"Vessel Omega has not reached the appropriate level of purification yet," answered Mother.

Margo had always been smarter than Susie; at least everyone seemed to think so. Susie had always seen how their father would talk to Margo about more complicated concepts—political, scientific—than he would with Susie. Or at least, in a different tone. It seemed like their father trusted Margo to just naturally understand things, even though she was the younger sister. This was the first time Susie had achieved something first, or better. Mother handed her a wooden spoon. Then Mother closed her eyes and moved her hands over the bowl, whispering syllables that Susie couldn't make out. When Mother opened her eyes, she spoke in her regular voice again.

"Now, you must take small bites, and masticate carefully, fifty times each mouthful. Your vessel body will need to adjust to digestion again." It was some kind of starchy mush with salt sprinkled on it. But as she ate, Susie could feel energy surging through her. Her mind calmed. She made sure to chew each bite fifty times. As she chewed, the gruel began almost to taste sweet. The energy throbbed in her cells. Was this the Power touching her?

15

Barbie and Ken loved playing good cop/bad cop. Especially with clever prey. Not that they were cops, nothing close to it. It's a turn of phrase, you know. But they sure were good at the game.

Paddy Skulldug had his silver cowboy boots up on his desk. His legs were splayed. He chewed on a mahogany-colored cigarillo. He didn't sweat easy.

"I told you," he said. "I run a legit business here. Print, DVDs, toys, interactive software. I don't traffic, don't deal with traffickers, and don't do anything illegal. I'm clean and clear."

"Paddy, gee, thanks. We really appreciate your help," said Ken.

"Ken, you wimp," said Barbie. "Let me handle this. Paddy, you don't seem to realize how serious this matter is. How would you like to do time?"

"I've done it already," said Paddy, rolling up his shiny red sleeve and flashing them his crooked blue Shirley tattoo.

"I'm not talking that bullshit six months in the county pen," said Barbie. "I'm talking real time. Upperstate. The Island. You know the kind of motherfuckers they've got locked up in that joint."

"Now, now, Barbie," said Ken. "No need to alarm him."
She snorted and crossed her arms.

"Look, Paddy, we're just trying to help you."

"Why?" said Paddy, and Barbie and Ken knew then that they had a chance with him. "I mean," Paddy added, "I don't need your help."

"You're right," said Ken. "I'm really sorry to have taken your time."

"This is bullshit," said Barbie. "I fucking hate dealing with those Fed assholes."

"I know, honey," said Ken. "But Paddy can take care of himself."

That was Barbie's cue to pace. So she paced back and forth a few times, sucking on a cigarette, her patent-leather overcoat swishing and her stilettos hammering the ugly linoleum floor. On one wall was a rack of DVDs, crappy-quality videos demonstrating every perversion you can imagine. On another wall were magazine and book racks. Stupid, flimsy fake whips and oils that got hot when you blew on them and purple dildos filled the shelves that ran down the middle of the store. Through the one-way mirrored windows, she could see the parking lot. A few minutes earlier, a would-be customer had pulled up and pulled on the door. But they had made Paddy lock up when they'd arrived, of course. Barbie really liked one-way mirrors. On the outside, she could gaze at her loveliness, and from the inside she could spy on people.

She turned back to Paddy and Ken.

"So," she said. "I guess you're not worried about the Samantha Butter case."

Paddy Skulldug lowered his silver boots from his desk, one and then the other. He leaned forward and squinted at Barbie. "Samantha Butter was a long time ago. I was a kid when that went down. Nobody ever proved I had anything to do with it. And if I did have something to do with it, I would have made my peace with the man upstairs. It would be between me and the good Lord. And that's *if* I had anything to do with it."

"Soooo," said Ken. "What happened the other day isn't worrisome to you?"

"Oh, forget it," said Barbie. "Ken, I thought we were going?"

"Wait," said Paddy. "What happened the other day?"

"Tuesday," said Ken.

"What was Tuesday?" said Paddy.

"Election Day, jackass," said Barbie.

"Oh, honey," said Ken. He licked his index finger and leaned over to rub a speck of dirt off his brown loafer. "Some people don't follow the news."

"Election Day?" said Paddy. "What the hell does that have to do with me? And Samantha Butter?"

"Did you see who was elected State Judge?" said Ken. Paddy shook his head.

"H. Mouse," said Barbie. "And H. Mouse is calling for a referendum to repeal the statute of limitations on manslaughter."

"Shit," said Paddy.

"Yeah," said Ken, sighing and shaking his head.

"Of course," Barbie said, "there are thousands of old, unsolved manslaughter cases. Arsons, hit-and-runs . . ."

"Drunken rowboat capsizings," added Ken.

"But they'll never get to all of them," said Barbie.

"So I'm sure there's nothing to worry about," said Ken.

"Unless . . ." Barbie's voice trailed off. This talk of manslaughter was making her hot. Maybe she'd help herself to one of those vinyl whips on the way out of this crudhole.

"Unless someone calls their attention to some specific old case," said Paddy, shaking his head.

"Samantha Butter was a gorgeous young girl in the prime of her life," said Ken.

"I'm sure there are people out there who haven't forgotten, even if her mother did commit suicide and her father moved down to Ciudad Boxico," said Barbie, feeling very proud of the way she pronounced the "x" in Boxico as an "h."

"They thought her dad might have done it," said Paddy. "Remember?"

"But then they totally cleared him," said Ken helpfully. "When his secretary came forward about the affair, remember?"

"Mr. Butter's semen on the Heartthrob Motel sheets," said Barbie, walking over to the end-cap display. She picked out a little red whip, lifted it off its hook, and whacked it against her thigh. It stung. She couldn't wait to get Ken alone and slap that silly, made-in-Taiwan toy against his hard, round buttocks.

Paddy's head was in his hands now. Ken admired Barbie's pert pink lips across the desk.

"Okay, okay," said Paddy without looking up. "I'll help. What do you need to know?"

"Oh, wow, man," said Ken. "Thank you so much!"

16

Here it was: the moment he had been working toward as long as he could remember. H. stared grimly through his windshield as he drove to the capitol, where he was to meet with the retiring State Judge whose job he was taking over. Then he was scheduled to have lunch with a reporter from the *State Eagle*, the region's largest and most serious newspaper. He could recite his campaign promises in his sleep: equality, parity, sanity, integrity. He was the outsider, the judge who had worked his way up through the ranks. The good father. His campaign pamphlets had shown him flanked by his two adorable daughters. Susie, trying to look grown-up in her navy-blue dress and matching bonnet; Margo smiling and saluting in the eyelet dress and ear bows that she loved. Tears blurred H. Mouse's vision and he wiped them away, sniffling a little. He tried to focus on the thruway. He was only at Exit 18. A long half hour still to drive. Maybe nothing bad had happened to Margo and Susie, he thought. But he knew that thought was as false as when he'd turned over to wake his wife up and shaken her and shaken her and for one second had told himself, *she's just sleeping very deeply.*

It started to drizzle. He turned on the wipers and then blotted his tears on his cuff. He pushed in the switch for the radio and fiddled with the knob until he found a classical music station. He came in at the last notes of a symphony. A honey-voiced announcer told him the name of the composer. A slow piano concerto began next. The tune was clear and simple. The notes wormed into his chest like parasites. He saw Margo and Susie, last Christmas Eve; the picture hovered right outside the car over the highway. There they were, pressed next to each other on the piano bench, bent over in concentration, playing Mozart.

17

Why was Susie looking at her so weirdly? Margo's stomach growled. She couldn't think clearly.

Their father always told them that there was no such thing as evil. He said that everyone was born good, that it was natural to be kind and giving. Their father said that empathy wasn't even a learned attribute, it was instinct, grown from evolutionary necessity. We needed empathy to survive, he said to his daughters. Yes, basic goodness, natural kindness and empathy could be trampled upon. By poverty. By drugs and alcohol. By the perversion of desire. But everybody, given support and the room to grow and breathe, was good.

Once, on a day of blinding sunlight, Margo had seen one of her classmates, hold a magnifying glass over an anthill in the schoolyard. A whole colony of ants—generations, the babies, the grandpas, the powerful, and the weak—died in the holocaust. She had smelled their charred corpses; she had seen the smoke rising in thin black columns. Margo remembered meeting Kyle's parents at the science fair, and they seemed perfectly fine. The mother had sweetly asked questions about Margo's salinithoscope, and the father had his arm around his wife. Kyle's older brother, Derrick, was in Susie's class, and he was pretty much one of the nicest students in the school. He was a star on the mumblety-peg team, but he was kind and friendly to everybody, even the nerds and the outcasts. No, Kyle was just bad, he was bad to the core, and there was no observable reason for his badness.

What Margo had sensed emanating from the dark hills was a deeper, scarier kind of bad than Kyle's, though. The Sunshine Family were hollow, Margo thought: it was like they had nothing inside them. It was like they were empty and needed to be filled. But they would never be filled. They would just continue stalking and consuming like zombies, all the while spewing that blather about the Power and hieroglyphics.

After she came in from looking at the unremarkable water spigot with Girl Sunshine, Margo went to sit next to Susie on the little woolen mat they'd been sharing. Susie had one of Father Sunshine's booklets (mimeographed, hand-stapled) on her lap. After shooting Margo a quick, strange glance, Susie had gone back to concentrating on it. Her brow was furrowed and her mouth was moving as she read. Margo could hear the sounds of Mother Sunshine doing something in the kitchen. Father and Boy were still outside on their patrol. Girl Sunshine was standing with her back to Margo and Susie, looking out of one of the van's groovy circular windows.

"Sobbusobbie," whispered Margo. That was Susie's name in Obby, their secret language.

Susie shot her a quick look. "Shhh," she said. Margo

finally recognized her weird expression. Susie was hiding something from Margo. Susie looked guilty.

"We have to get out of here," whispered Margo, still speaking in Obby. "I'm starving. And Daddy—" She stopped, shaking her head and feeling nauseous. Their poor father.

"You need to pay better attention to the Ordinations," said Susie, a little louder and not in Obby. "We are destined for something more amazing than we can even imagine."

Margo looked up at her sister. She gazed into her eyes and Susie gazed right back. Margo couldn't tell if Susie was acting or if she had really started to believe in the Sunshine Family's fictions. Margo leaned forward and sniffed her sister's breath. She didn't smell sour like she had before; she smelled like food. Margo squinted at Susie. She still had no idea what was going on inside her sister's head. But she knew what she had to do if she didn't want to starve to death.

THREE

18

Barbie propped the pink princess phone between her chin and shoulder. Sitting there at the white vanity table, she watched herself talking in the mirror. Her pointed feet were soaking in a small tub of bubble-gum-scented suds. Skipper stood behind her, carefully pulling Barbie's pink comb through her long blonde locks. Barbie watched herself talking, but she could see Skipper there behind her—in her red jumper and white blouse, little chest bumps just barely poking out through the cloth.

Skipper in turn watched Barbie as she talked on the phone. Barbie was pretending to be something she wasn't, which Skipper knew was part of the job. If Barbie and Ken didn't pretend, Skipper wouldn't have this fabulous life, with the pool and the palm trees and the vistas. Skipper never had to pretend anything.

"Yes, I have the directions," said Barbie. "Yes, we'll be there at ten tonight. Yes, I have the password. Yes, we know to bring cash for the tires. Yes, it will just be the two of us."

After she hung up, Skipper said, "Tires?"

Barbie looked up at Skipper's face in the mirror. "It's a code word."

"For what?" asked Skipper.

"Juvenile property. Trade."

"Slaves?" said Skipper. She spritzed some hairspray on Barbie's mane.

"Yup," said Barbie. She yawned. "Have you seen Ken? I feel like having sex."

"Oh, he's out on the deck, doing his exercises."

Barbie removed her feet from their bath and went over to the dressing-room window. Below, she could see Ken in the middle of his daily calisthenics. With his right arm, he removed his left arm and placed it next to him on a mat. Then he removed his left leg, followed by his right one. He liked to focus on his core muscles first. Barbie rubbed her hand between her legs as she watched him do his one-armed crunches. Skipper sat down at the vanity table and tried on some of Barbie's pink lipstick. Barbie began to moan, rubbing harder and faster. When Barbie saw Ken beginning to reinsert his limbs, she ran out of the dressing room.

Skipper admired her bright pink painted lips in the mirror. She fluffed her hair and jutted out her chest. She tried rubbing between her legs like Barbie, but nothing happened. So she wandered over to the window and looked down at the deck.

Barbie was smoking a cigarette, reclining on one of the lounge chairs with her negligee pushed up past her navel. Ken, whose left arm still lay on the mat, was pulling one of Barbie's legs off. Then he picked up his free arm and slowly moved it, hand first, into the Barbie's empty leg joint. Skipper saw Barbie arch her back and drag deeply on the cigarette. Kneeling before her on his bendable legs, Ken moved the arm in and out of Barbie's pelvic cavity. Skipper closed the curtain and went back downstairs to the deluxe kitchen. It seemed like a good time to make a tray of cupcakes.

19

When Father Sunshine and Boy came back in from their patrols, Margo walked right over to Father and knelt at his feet. Something cold and determined had settled into her heart. She was alone in this ugly game.

"Father," she said.

He looked surprised. "Yes, Vessel Omega?"

"I have been thinking about the prophesies."

"You have?"

"Yes. I have been meditating on the Dodecahedron."

"This is great news, Vessel Omega."

Margo nodded her head, bowing a little and doing her best to convey absolute deference.

"I just wanted to let you know that I look forward to learning more about the hieratic ordinations."

She glanced around the cramped van. Did the Sunshine children exchange looks, or was it her imagination?

Susie appeared and knelt down next to Margo. "I look forward to it, too," she said. Margo tried to decode her tone of voice, but it was unreadable.

The old judge and his aide had shown H. Mouse around the offices of the Justice Building. The office that would soon be his overlooked a small park with a fountain, a bronze statue of the Founder of the Courts, and some cherry trees—which were of course now bare and spindly. Next to an impressive collection of diplomas and certificates, the old judge had pictures on his wall, posed portraits of his family: his matronly wife, who had wrinkly ears and a long nose; his five offspring and their many progeny, all dressed up for some formal occasion. H. Mouse had waddled over to the desk and touched the green blotter paper.

"Go ahead," the old judge had said in his creaky voice, eyes twinkling. "Try it out." He gestured at the desk chair with his cane.

H. Mouse had sat down at the desk then, and he felt completely split in two. Half of him was absorbing the enormity of responsibility that he had not just voluntarily accepted but actively pursued. Had he been crazy, he wondered. The other half of him reeled and spun, dizzy with terror and guilt. His poor little daughters. Would he ever be able to have their portraits taken and hang them on the sober gray wallpaper?

The old judge patted H.'s shoulder. "I know, son. I know. The gravity of sitting at that desk for the first time."

H. nodded. "It's powerful," he said, choking back a sob.

"You're ready," the old one had said. He'd moved around the desk and sat across from H. He'd leaned in toward his replacement. "You know, I probably wouldn't have chosen to retire this year if I hadn't gotten wind of your plans to run. I knew you were the only one besides me who could beat the other guy. And I knew you had the integrity and perspective to carry out the duties of this job."

Now H. Mouse was standing outside Harrigan's Pub, waiting for the journalist. A taxi pulled up, and out hopped Liz Fox. He recognized her from the picture next to her byline in the *Eagle*. She was more lively in real life, he thought. And younger than he expected. She was wearing a form-fitting black coat. Her black eyes flashed at him when she greeted him. And she was certainly not shy. In an almost masculine gesture, she pushed open the door of Harrigan's and held it open.

H. Mouse had been to the pub once or twice before. Really it wasn't a pub but a pubbish expensive restaurant frequented by lawyers and politicians. Tiffany lamps with dim bulbs hung low over the intimate tables, which were placed far enough apart that eavesdropping was difficult. The floor was carpeted and the chairs densely cushioned. Harrigan's was famous for its blue-cheese steak and stiff drinks. H. reminded himself to be careful.

"It's such a pleasure to meet you," said Liz to H., after the maitre d' had taken her coat and pulled a chair out for her. "I've been following your career for a while."

"Yes," he said. "I know. Thank you for the attention you helped us get for the school lunch case last year."

"Oh, you know," she said, "I'm not advocating for anyone or anything. I'm an unbiased member of the press."

She laughed. Her black eyes seemed to slant up when she smiled. A waiter came to take their drink orders.

"Dirty martini," said Liz.

H. was about to order what he really wanted, which was a scotch, double, on the rocks. But then he stopped himself. Drinking, and the inhibitions it loosened, had gotten him into trouble in the past. He pushed the image of Barbie and Ken, that midnight drive a couple years ago, and the briefcase full of cash, out of his head. "Club soda with a slice of lime."

When they were alone again, Liz Fox pulled a tape recorder out of a bulging black bag. As she fiddled with a microphone and some batteries, she said, "I didn't know that H. Mouse, State Judge—elect, was a teetotaler."

"Oh, I'm not," said H. quickly. "It's just that I'm on antibiotics for a, um, an eye thing, conjunctivitis, that is. Can't drink. Certainly not if I'm to drive home." He patted his tummy, having no idea why he did so.

"Gotcha," said Liz Fox. "So, is it cool with you if I turn this on now?"

He nodded.

She asked the usual puff questions he'd expected: would he still have time for the community work with his neighbors, was he going to redecorate the office, and how did his daughters feel about his win? (He had practiced an answer for this one in front of the mirror, but still he winced when he gave it.) About half an hour into the interview, their salads came, Liz Fox ordered a second martini, and H. Mouse asked for a ginger ale. Sipping her fresh drink, Liz pushed the microphone a little closer to him and said, "So, Mr. Mouse. There's a reason you're so well liked. Your messages of equality, integrity, and parity have really resonated across many districts and demographics. Your grassroots campaigning appealed to both young folks and the older ones who remembered a time when politics was simpler and more meaningful and politicians really accomplished things. But there's one issue that I—and many others, even many of your supporters—am confused about your position on . . ." She gestured with a swizzle stick upon which three olives were impaled. "And that's this whole repeal-the-statute-of-limitations thing for manslaughter cases."

H. Mouse shuddered. "Ah, yes," he said. He took a breath, let it out. He'd learned in his days as a lawyer and then attorney that it was sometimes good to just let people keep talking rather than jump in too soon.

After a moment, Liz Fox continued: "Well, in general you're seen as so fair. Pretty liberal without being radical."

"Uh huh." H.'s heart was racing.

"Well, I just don't understand. I mean, even if someone did cause someone's death two decades ago—say, in a hit-and-run when they were a teenager, or out hunting and accidentally hitting the wrong target, or because they were all hopped up on caffeine at the time and didn't know what they were doing—but like I said, it's been two decades, why dig up the old wounds? Why go after them if they've never killed again? If they've matured and had full lives? Don't you think that if they're basically good and mean well—and isn't that what you believe? That we are all basically good?—why punish them if so much time has passed?"

"Hmm," said H. He took a sip of ginger ale, and was grateful that he hadn't ordered scotch.

Liz slid an olive off the swizzle stick with her sharp little teeth. Her nose twitched. "Some citizens thought that maybe you took that stance to get the backing of certain groups, crime-victim groups that normally wouldn't support a candidate as liberal as yourself."

"Ah," said H., nodding.

Liz flipped a page of her memo pad. "For instance, Offspring of the Mugged, Association for the Return of Separated Limbs and Digits, United Organization of Poaching Sufferers . . ." She gnawed another olive and gazed across the table at H.

He took a bite of salad and chewed it slowly. Then he spoke: "Well, Liz. I appreciate the question and I'm grateful for the chance to articulate my position to your readers. Yes, I do believe we're all good. Not one of us is born bad, and there's no such thing as evil. If a citizen has killed someone, no matter how long ago, and they haven't paid penance of some sort, they are still living with their guilt—most likely secretly. I imagine it's a very lonely place to be, a very sad and dark place. And I imagine that, given that there's goodness at everyone's core, they wish to say they're sorry but they don't know how."

Liz Fox nodded. H. went on: "Now, it's natural to be scared of punishment. Most folks don't have the unbelievable courage it takes to come forward and say, 'I've done something bad.' A repeal of that statute of limitations would simply give those who've done something terrible in the past a chance to do the right thing. To pay the proper price and then move forward with their lives, never to live in shame and darkness again."

He still had it. Even under stress he could still do it. He hadn't wept, hadn't pounded the table. Hadn't sounded defensive. Liz was smiling at him.

"Thanks so much for the clarification," she said. She reached over and cupped his cheek, which H. found startling but not unpleasant. "I think that's enough for this interview."

21

"Thus the Power enters my vessel body, and thus the Power gives me strength. As the Dodecahedron was in the First Days, so is it now. The Dodecahedron is constant, the pulp of the vessel is weak. So why does the Power grant its Spirit Carriers these Vessel Bodies?"

"To fulfill the prophecies and distribute the Ordinations?"

"Yes, Vessel Omega."

Girl Sunshine swiveled her head. Margo could feel Girl's cold, dull gaze, sweeping up and down Margo's body.

"Vessel Omega, in what form will the Power signal that the momentum has begun?"

"Thirty hours of darkness, Father."

"And then, Vessel Omega . . . ?"

Margo opened her mouth to speak again, but Susie blurted, breathless: "The prophecies!"

"Vessel Alpha, I was querying Vessel Omega." Father hinged an arm up and pointed at the corner of the van. "The Power commands you to Rest."

"Yes, Father," said Susie.

Margo kept her head locked squarely in place, but in her peripheral vision she saw her sister, quivering a little, move toward their blanket.

"Vessel Omega, what sound will we Vessels hear when the Darkness lifts and the Fulfillment commences?"

"Hissing. The hissing of serpents."

Father Sunshine hovered his hand over Margo's head. "Yes, Vessel Omega. Girl, you may take Vessel Omega to the spigot now."

Condensation clouded the van's windows. It was dusk. Outside the tin cans rattled on the line.

Margo heard the scratchy sound of Girl's hip hinges as girl stood up. Margo stood and followed her out of the van. It was drizzling. This was her third or fourth time going to the spigot with Girl. Standing there in the mist as the icy water rushed into the bucket and splashed on her legs, Margo thought about shaking Girl. She wanted to punish her, interrogate her, show her something real. She imagined stomping on one of Girl's hands and commanding her to admit that she felt pain.

But Margo knew better. Margo cranked the spigot shut. Girl reached for the handle of the bucket. Their eyes met. They stood like that for a while, and it felt to Margo like a dare. She broke away first. Girl picked up the bucket.

22

It had stopped raining. It was rush hour. H. Mouse was halfway home; driving in the right lane along with the commuters who peeled off at every exit. He imagined they were all returning to happy, safe offspring and comforting spouses. He felt the sweat begin to bead behind his ears. But then, couldn't he take a little credit if they *were* going home to security and prosperity? In his district, anyway? He'd been a good village councilor. And now he had won this election, fair and square. One week from today, he would be H. Mouse, State Judge. And in his new post, all of these citizens would be a part of his greater family. He had a responsibility to them.

Again, he commended himself for not ordering that scotch he'd wanted. He went over the moment in his head: when Liz Fox had asked him about the statute of limitations, he had waited. He hadn't jumped to the defensive. He'd let her explain her question. She hadn't been probing into his association with Mr. Glet at all, as it turned out. Not that he had done anything illegal there. But it just seemed best not to broadcast.

When Mr. Glet invited him over to smoke cigars and drink port; when Mr. Glet told H. the story of what had happened twenty years ago, how Mrs. Glet was tripped on the real electric escalator that really went up and down at Lucky's; when Mr. Glet explained how a witness had finally come forward just three months after the statute of limitations had expired—a witness who had seen the long umbrella dangling from the killer's gloved fist; when Mr. Glet's eyes welled up as he explained that this witness was not allowed to submit testimony; when Mr. Glet announced with a tremor in his voice that he knew H. was the only one who had the integrity to set things straight with this manslaughter problem; when Mr. Glet suggested H. set up a consultancy firm and "advise" Mr. Glet on "civic matters"; when the checks started coming in, far above the limit on campaign contributions, made out to "HM, LLC" and signed "P. I. Glet": the law had not actually been broken. Still, it had seemed counterproductive to bring the public's attention to the arrangement. H. and Mr. Glet had agreed on this point.

H. had practiced what he would say if a reporter or opponent had stumbled upon it, and he'd even felt satisfied that it wasn't technically not the truth: over the course of the past year, he had become friendly with one of his constituents and learned his tragic story; they had gotten to know each other while H. Mouse was doing some consulting work for him; through casual conversations, H. had had his mind changed about manslaughter—and so, yes, while there was an indirect connection between his friendship with P. I. Glet and his pressing for a change to the law, nothing untoward had happened. But, thank goodness, he still hadn't needed to give that speech.

H. signaled and turned onto the curved exit ramp. For a moment, he had forgotten everything, and he felt the usual swell in his heart that came when he'd been away from his daughters for a few hours and was returning home to them. But by the time he got to the end of the ramp, he remembered. And the agony set in once again.

23

Barbie knew that others had the kinds of jobs where they woke up at the same time every day, arrived at the office at 8:59 a.m., talked about lunch with their coworkers, packed up their briefcases at 5:30 p.m., and forgot about work until the next morning at 8:59 a.m. Barbie didn't pay taxes; she had five driver's licenses—all bearing different names—and three passports; she woke up at a different time every day, and sometimes she didn't sleep at all. She liked it this way. What was it to be part of the system, arriving and leaving as predictably as the second hand on a clock? Why, to be one of those drones was to be practically dead. Barbie chose to feel alive. Yes, her life included danger. A lot of it. But being in danger made her appreciate the moment, made her appreciate life's simple pleasures like sunny days, pretty clothes, good food, and having her orifices penetrated.

Barbie and Ken stood outside of the low warehouse building on the edge of the canal. They'd been buzzed in at the front gate and patted down by a couple of thugs in a decrepit trailer. Now they were waiting for the head of the whole operation.

He came out wearing camo and a beret, silver heart pinned on his chest.

He shook their hands. Didn't even glance at Barbie's chest bumps, which surprised her. He stood rigidly straight. Barbie could practically see his six-pack through his tight shirt.

"Corporal Joe," said Barbie.

"Ben, Karly," he said. "You can just call me G.I. Only ones who call me Corporal are my bodyguards and the product."

"Where is the product?" asked Ken.

"I'd like to talk in my office first. There are some business matters I like to go over with new clients before we get started. Standard stuff."

They followed him across the dirt yard and into the warehouse. First they passed through a dark foyer; then a heavy sliding door opened before them, revealing a fluorescent-lit room with a big gray desk, filing cabinets, a black phone with a blinking light, and a few chairs. It looked like any warehouse office, Barbie thought.

"Have a seat," said G.I. They sat. "Coffee?"

"No, thanks," said Barbie.

G.I. picked up the black receiver and pushed a button on the phone. "Pam, may we have the standard registration materials?"

A minute later, Pam arrived. She was short and chubby, wearing an ochre pantsuit. Her hair was badly permed, Barbie thought, and her makeup was all wrong. She had on orthopedic shoes that laced up the sides. She handed G.I. Joe a manila folder and shuffled out of the room.

G.I. opened the folder and took a ballpoint pen out of his breast pocket. "So," he said. "I know my assistants screened you ahead of time, but for my records here, who did you say referred you?"

"Paddy Skulldug," said Ken.

"Good guy," said G.I. "And how much product did you have in mind, Karly?"

"Two, maybe three . . . ," said Barbie.

"Great. Now, do looks matter?"

"What do you mean?" asked Barbie.

"Well, you know, depending on your intended use, the appearance may or may not be important."

"Oh, I see. No, looks don't matter," said Barbie. For a second she thought it would be nice to give a sexy little slave to Ken for Valentine's Day. But then she reminded herself that they weren't doing this for fun. They were here on H. Mouse's dime.

G.I. checked a box.

"Age? Preferred range, that is?"

"Young," said Ken.

"The choices we offer are: (a) juvenile, (b) pubescent or young adolescent, (c) late adolescent, or (d) fully grown."

"A," said Barbie. "Juvenile."

"Alrighty," said G.I. Joe. "I like to develop good relations with my customers. Most return to do business again. So, are there any questions that you have for me? Obviously I can't answer everything, but I can talk about our procedures here. Oh, also, I should let you know, too, that this"—he pointed to a mirror affixed to the wall behind him—"is a camera, that the room is miked, and that five of my biggest guys are standing outside right now."

"Is it okay if I smoke?" asked Barbie, reaching into her patent-leather purse.

"No," said Joe.

"I have a question," said Ken. "It's really just curiosity on my part, but how did you get into this business?"

"Well, Ben, I'm glad you asked, because the answer may surprise you. When I was down in the jungle fighting the war, you wouldn't believe the suffering I saw. In the villages, in the swamplands, and in the nomadic encampments, everywhere these pretty little things were caught in the violence, starving and desperate. The insurgents used their bodies like meat, and some of the Democratic Liberation officers weren't much better, I'm sorry to say. I figured, there's got to be a way to help them. When my tour was done I tried to set up an aid foundation, but in spite of my Purple Heart, no one would give me the time of day. So I had to start a clandestine business, bringing these victims here and placing them in new homes."

As Joe gave his little speech, Barbie noticed that his knee was jiggling under his desk and he kept licking his lips. What a pile of bull dung, thought Barbie. Did anyone believe this crap about the noble soldier? She didn't care about the origin of his wares, but she hated a bad liar. Her little crush on him had completely dissolved.

"That is a wonderful story," said Barbie. "May we see your selection now?"

"Yes, Karly, but as you know, I need to keep a deposit, whether or not you wind up actually purchasing something today. It's for security reasons."

Ken opened the briefcase and placed a pile of bills on Joe's desk.

A minute later they were walking across the foyer again. They boarded a freight elevator, and when the rear doors opened there were two huge guards waiting there. They flanked Joe as he led Barbie and Ken to a catwalk.

"Here we are," said Joe. "These twelve suites are our juveniles."

The suites were wire cages, each with a few mattresses on the floor. Their occupants sure didn't look like they came from the jungle. And most of them looked miserable, even catatonic. Probably drugged. In the first Barbie saw one of them pushing a small red ball back and forth. Next to her, another chewed on her own toe. Neither looked up. In the second cage, one of the captives ran up to them, slamming against the metal, smiling desperately, batting her eyes and wiggling her rear end. In yet another cage, three were piled in a heap, asleep or passed out.

"They're all healthy," said Joe. "They've had their vaccinations, and they've been checked for diseases. They're a good product."

Barbie liked H. Mouse. Liked him more than most of their clients. Even though she had been hoping this would be a quick job, in and out, she was relieved that she wouldn't have to tell H. that his daughters had been in this horrible place. She was pretty sure that Joe's wards never recovered.

The plan had been to walk away if Margo and Susie weren't here. But back in Joe's office, Barbie decided to take a huge chance. If it got her and Ken in trouble, well, life was full of trouble if you lived it right.

"Joe . . . ," Barbie said. She really wanted a cigarette.

"I'm getting the feeling that none of the juveniles suited you. Are you sure you're not looking for the next age-level up? The pubescents tend to be more lively."

"I have to level with you, G.I.," said Barbie. Ken looked over at her. "We're not looking to purchase random juveniles. We're looking for two specific ones who disappeared last week." She turned her gaze to the mirror on the wall and addressed the camera. G.I. reached for something under his desk. Barbie leaned forward and touched his arm. "We're not cops. Far from it. We operate in the same shadow world as you do, friend. Right now, in fact, we're working for someone who has hired us specifically to avoid the scrutiny of the law. And his daughters were taken from him. Since they're not here, I thought maybe you could give us some leads for where else to look. And then we can all pretend we never met."

24

Margo and her father had always had a special connection. She knew him, she knew him so well. People said she was like him, that she resembled him. Even though they were close, it wasn't actually the case that Margo was so much like him. Sometimes he seemed like the young one to her, and she felt old, as if she were the grown-up. She'd never known her mother, and she sensed that in some roundabout way she'd become her own mother— and by extension, her father's helpmate. Sometimes she thought H. was naïve and needed protection. Her poor dad, how he took everything to heart. He himself had no idea, really, how fragile he was—and sometimes, when she looked at her father across the room at a library fund-raiser or teatime meet and greet for his constituents, she half expected him to crumple into a helpless and rumpled pile of cloth, like a pillowcase that's been left in the dryer. Nobody else seemed to notice, though. Her father seemed to have the magic touch with the citizens. Margo thought that maybe what she saw as helpless and vulnerable in her father translated into sincere and real for the voters. That's what they always said about her dad in articles and editorials: he's *real*.

Margo knew, she *knew*, that her father was in agony right now. She knew the kind of angst and guilt and fear he was experiencing. She knew he wouldn't be able to function for very long without her and Susie at his side. She figured he'd probably won the election, and it broke her heart to imagine him unable to celebrate. Her father was proud. He also had a certain shyness, which he pretended was determination and ambition. And he was vigilant about maintaining his public image. Margo figured he hadn't told the police about the fact that she and Susie were missing. Not even Bub Flytrap.

But how would he find them without the police? She didn't want to think about it. Once, when she came home from school a little early, she'd heard her father whispering inside the coat closet. Another time, he said he was going to be at the office all day until late, working on the plastics recycling expansion proposal—but when she called him to tell him she'd gotten an A+ on the earth science quiz, the receptionist said he'd only dropped by for a few minutes that morning to pick up his mail and messages. Margo was aware that, while she knew her father very, very well, she didn't know everything about him. And she was glad she didn't.

These were Margo's thoughts as she recited the twelve Elemental Ordinations.

"Thus the Power commands: that the serpent swallows its own venom and grows stronger; that the scorpion stings its vessel; that the stags locks antler to antler." Father Sunshine intoned the Third Ordination. He was wearing his black poncho and white hood.

"Serpent, venom; scorpion, stings; stag, antler," answered Susie, Margo and Boy and Girl Sunshine. They all kneeled on a mat at his feet.

Father Sunshine inhaled. "Thus the Power commands: that the avalanche buries the rot; that the snowdrift smothers the poison; that the flood swallows the putrescence of flesh."

"Avalanche, rot; snowdrift, poison; flood, flesh," they answered.

Margo looked sideways at Susie. Susie's eyes were closed, and she was wearing an alien smile, a version of the ones the Sunshine Family wore on their shiny beige faces. Margo felt that bitter twist. Her sister really was this weak. Where was Susie's conscience, her consciousness? Sometimes, here in the van, Margo thought maybe she didn't love Susie anymore. She saw Susie differently now. If they ever got out of this, Susie would be the kind that gives herself to the first suitor to tell her she's pretty. She'd be the kind that orders products off the television. She'd be the kind that would join an angry mob.

Were they already up to the Eighth Ordination? Margo's mouth kept moving.

She glanced up and out, through the circular window.

It was always dark here on the mountain, deep in the trees. Their branches and dense foliage made a constant twilight, and the icy wind shuddered across the clearing, riling little twisters of dust and pine needles.

"Thus the Power commands," chanted Father Sunshine. He kept his voice perfectly flat. Margo had heard Susie practicing, trying to hit the same kind of flatness."—that the sun shall go dark for twelve moons; that the sands absorb the air; that the hieroglyphics are restored to the vessels' pyramidal tracts."

It was the final ordination. Margo recited the response along with the others. She squeezed her eyes shut to look extra devout. She sat up straight and bobbed her head and pretended she was experiencing blissful transcendence.

Afterwards, Father Sunshine commended her chanting: "I could see the Power vibrations pulsating in your vessel body, Vessel Omega," he said. "You are getting closer and closer to the next level of purity."

"Thank you, Father," she said, lowering her eyes.

How easy it was to pretend. How easy it was to separate her inside and outside, to make her limbs and voice and face behave one way, while her mind and heart were somewhere else completely.

Maybe she was like her father, very much like her father, after all.

25

Skipper flipped the pages of a magazine as she ate her bowl of fruit cocktail. She always picked out the maraschino cherries first, and often didn't even touch the grapefruit. It was sunny and hot out on the deck. The parrots chattered in the palm trees. She looked at the pictures in the magazine and imagined she was also in a picture in a magazine. She could see the picture: Skipper on the deck, in her plaid dress and bare feet, eating fruit salad, flipping the pages of a magazine, and imagining herself in a picture.

26

The young clerk, Benjy Weevil, was clearly nervous around the newly elected State Judge. H. Mouse knew that Benjy had been an intern until a couple of months before, and that working under H. would be his first job with real responsibilities. Benjy Weevil didn't smell very good. H. hoped it was just due to anxiety, and that the odor would go away once the clerk relaxed into his job.

H. had noticed that his own body wasn't behaving right. He didn't smell the way he should, either. He was running to the bathroom often; he'd found a private one in the basement of the Justice Building. He couldn't eat very much at a sitting, and he was losing weight. The other judges and the State Attorney joked about his nerves: they'd all been through it, they said: the adrenaline, the insomnia. They called it "the swearing-in diet." "To take off all the weight you gained at those county fairs and banquets during the campaign," said Justice Lynx, whose policies H. Mouse despised, but whom he couldn't help but like for her slinky walk and insouciant sense of humor.

He hadn't officially started the job yet, thank goodness. No, he was just having some boxes and files moved in while the old judge and his aides packed up. The court was on a break, the State Legislature was on a recess. There were some briefing meetings to attend, some lessons to learn on navigating the culture of the Justice Building. He walked through all of this as if he were being programmed by some unseen remote control. Somehow he was able to function, even as the picture of his daughters throbbed inside his skull like a headache.

Sometimes he went down to the private bathroom in the basement even when he didn't need to use it. He'd lower the toilet cover and sit on it, just trying to breathe and make reason of things. He thought of Margo most often. It was she who he stood to betray, to disappoint. He couldn't bear the idea of falling down in front of her. If something happened to Margo, if he didn't find her in time to prevent some irreversible damage, she would never forgive him, and then, well, then he would just have to die. With Susie it was different: it's not that he loved his elder daughter any less, it was simply that they spoke a different language. He knew that Susie's mind worked in a different way from his and Margo's. Susie would be fine, even if she wasn't. And Margo might not be fine, even if she was.

Two days earlier, Barbie had called his private line, the one his daughters didn't know about, the one in the coat closet. She had spoken in vague terms, but he was pretty sure about what she'd meant: that there was progress. On one hand, he hated the thought that his daughters' lives might be dependent on Barbie and Ken. On the other hand,

Barbie and Ken had never let him down. He trusted them. He paid for that trust, paid handsomely, but still it was trust.

27

Barbie handed Olga Schevschenko the cheap vinyl travel bag. The alley smelled like rotting orange rinds and pig offal. Barbie was wearing a black wig and a trench coat. She looked hot, like a hot spy. Sounds from the restaurant— dishes clattering, water running, cooks and waiters shouting and joking—buried Olga and Barbie's brief conversation. Barbie knew that Olga Schevschenko was not her real name, no more than Barbie's name was Angela Goldentwig. Barbie knew Olga's accent was probably just as fake as Barbie's. It didn't matter, so long as her information was real, as real as the money in the cheap vinyl travel bag.

Olga passed Barbie a worn manila envelope. "The details are in here," she said, in that ridiculous accent. "I'm not doing this for the money," she added.

Barbie took out a cigarette and placed it in her long, lacquered cigarette holder, which she thought was a really nice touch. She French-inhaled. As the smoke curled away from her, she said, "Of course not."

"There are scattered settlements across the country, especially on the far coast. They tend to encamp in the mountains, and they'll watch a community for a long time before deciding who to take."

Barbie nodded. "How do they decide?"

"It's all in the papers. I've given you some of their original mimeographs. Their decisions are based on messages they think they're getting from the Power."

Barbie snorted. "The *Power?*"

Olga didn't smile. Grimly she asked, "Have you ever dealt with true believers before?"

Barbie couldn't even imagine what that meant. She shook her head.

"They are the most dangerous of all. Be wary if you find them. They will not think twice about giving their own lives, or taking anyone else's, if they're convinced it's what their scriptures tell them to do."

Barbie nodded, trying to take it in. The lowlife scum she was used to confronting might care about nothing but themselves; however, they did care about themselves.

"True believers, Angela, are like a virus. Be forewarned." And then Olga turned and walked up the alley, over the cobblestones, through the oily steam spewing from the kitchen vents, and to the iron gate, which she slipped through as quietly as she had arrived.

FOUR

28

What's that? You think you'd get a little bit attached? You think you'd form some kind of emotional bond with them? You'd find them sort of cute when they were kneeling in front of you, echoing your words so seriously? Well, you're not Father Sunshine.

If you were Father Sunshine, you'd know: these Vessel Bodies—Alpha, Omega—are mere stuff, as ugly and utilitarian as the xylem and phloem of a tree or the jelly of a cactus. The life burning inside the spirit Carriers is so temporary, the fact that they're breathing and walking around is practically a form of galvanism. They're made of weak, gelatinous pulp that the Power has seen fit to briefly electrify with Its energy. Father Sunshine does not look at them and see Margo and Susie. No. He sees matter pulsating with the Power. He must teach them; he must pass on the Hieratic Ordinations; he must keep building the pyramid.

Before Father Sunshine, there was One. The One taught Father and Mother Sunshine. Father and Mother will pass on the Ordinations to the Four: Boy, Girl, Alpha and Omega. The Four will forge Eight. And so on. So on. High up on mountains everywhere, the Power will multiply and extend. Soon, soon, everything that is foul and tainted will be smothered by that which is righteous and pure.

Pure.

Nearly nothing is pure these days. Even in this mountain water spouting from this pump, as cold as it is, as clean as it seems, you can still taste the influence. The impurity. Look out across the valley here. You see those houses? The dots that are gas stations and convenience stores and medical office parks? These things are temporary, too. When the pyramid is built across mountainsides, the avalanche will rain down and bury the rot. So it is Ordained.

29

H. Mouse crouched in the coat closet. He was wedged in the corner, his somewhat sunken tummy pressed against his legs. It smelled like wool and camphor in there. And candy. One of his daughters must have stashed a gummy something in a jacket pocket and forgotten about it. His tear ducts were in constant contraction these days, in spasm.

"What have you found?" said H. "Please, please tell me you've got something for me." He wanted to say, *please tell me they're alive*, but every statement, once spoken aloud, implies the possibility of its counterpoint.

"I've got something, yes," said Barbie. He could hear a puff, as if she had just lit a cigarette. "A lead. I don't know how far this lead will take us."

"What is it? Oh please, tell me what it is." H. Mouse pictured himself kneeling at Barbie's arched feet, hugging her bendable legs, burying his head in her pink lap. At this moment she was his mother, his goddess, his petitionee.

"H., listen, I can't. I can't tell you."

"Why?"

"I can tell you this: the good news is that they're probably alive." She said it. "The bad news is, if we're right, this isn't a normal kidnapping—which we already figured, right?"

"Right," said H. Mouse. "No ransom note, no contact."

"But if this is what we think it is, this also isn't a normal abnormal kidnapping."

"What do you mean?" said H. Mouse. His heart was beating about fourteen times a second.

"I can't tell you. But it's going to take us a couple of days to put together a game plan. Until then, you just need to sit tight."

H. couldn't control his breathing. He'd been working so hard to hold himself together—with Liz Fox, Benjy Weevil, the old judge. He'd been telling the neighborhood acquaintances who'd dropped by to congratulate him that Margo and Susie were visiting an aunt. He'd told their teachers that they both had a bad flu. He couldn't do it anymore. He felt himself panting, getting dizzy.

"H.," said Barbie. "Calm down. Please. Don't hyper-ventilate."

H. kept panting.

"Breathe," said Barbie. "I want to hear you take a deep breath. Will you do that for me?"

H. took a breath.

"Okay, another. And slower this time."

H. took another, slower, breath.

"Good. Good job," said Barbie.

"My swearing in is in three days," said H. Mouse. "I really need to get them back before then."

"Oh, by the way, great article by Liz Fox," said Barbie.

"Thanks," said H. He took another deep breath before he said good-bye to Barbie and hung up the phone. Sitting there, on the carpet, he had a sense of disbelief. *Do I really only get one chance at this?* he asked himself. *I can't go back through my own story and change the outcome? Will I really never have the opportunity to undo everything I regret?*

30

Skipper stood under the eaves of the townhouse, slowly twirling her baton between two fingers. The day was, as always, hot and sunny, and she could hear the parrots chattering to each other down on the driveway.

She felt something, which was strange enough. But even stranger was the fact that she could name the feeling: *missing.* That was the word in her head. But every time the baton flipped over, she changed her mind. She couldn't decide if she was missing something, or if she was the one that was missing.

Skipper moved along the side of the house a little, to a spot where she could see Ken. He had his tool kit out and was hammering a nail into a board on the far end of the patio. Tap, tap, tap. His back was facing Skipper. She studied his broad shoulders and the seams where they met his arms. Then she studied the arms and their identical gleaming topographies of muscle.

Barbie was out doing something for their job, probably stocking up on weaponry. Skipper could tell this job was more important than most, because Barbie had been working extra hard. The last few nights, when Skipper went to bed, Barbie had still been up, practicing her quick draw in front of the mirror. Last night, Skipper had offered to help with the mission, and Barbie had said, "You know what would be really nice? If you built a beautiful sand castle with your pink bucket and shovel."

Ken didn't know Skipper was watching him right now. He finished hammering that nail and took another nail out of his tool kit. Skipper stepped out from the shade into the heat, still twirling, and approached Ken. When she reached him, she tapped him on the shoulder with her baton. He jumped a little and jerked his head up to look at her.

"Hi, Ken." Skipper gave a little curtsey.

"Oh, hi, Skipper. What's up?"

Skipper had known Ken would be surprised to see her there. They'd lived together for as long as Skipper could remember, but she couldn't recall the last time they had a conversation that didn't also include Barbie.

Skipper placed her baton on the ground. She reached up inside one of the short puffy sleeves of her blouse and tugged. Her arm came out of its hole. She turned sideways and presented the hole to Ken. She figured that he would put his hand in there, and it would feel good. It would be so good to have his hand in her armhole that she wouldn't feel *missing* anymore.

Ken put down his hammer and stood up. "No, no, Skipper," he said. "I can't do that with you."

"Why? What's wrong with me?"

"Nothing's wrong with you." He took her arm from her, and began to fit it back in its hole. "It's just, um . . . you're Skipper and I'm Ken, and that's why we can't do it."

"Barbie wouldn't care." Skipper pouted and kicked at her baton.

"I care," said Ken. He gave her arm one more push, and it popped into place. Then he patted her on the shoulder. "Why don't you go bake some cookies in your oven or something? Barbie will be home soon, and I bet she'll be real hungry."

Ken bent down, picked up the pink baton and passed it up to Skipper.

31

Susie—no, Vessel Alpha—Rested her body. Her Vessel Body, that is. She lay on her back on the van's plastic floor. Margo—Vessel Omega—was lying next to her. When she had further purified herself, Vessel Alpha would be given a piece of foam rubber, just like Boy and Girl had.

She went over the first Ordination in her head. Father Sunshine said it had always been in her mind, she had just forgotten it when her vessel body took this particular form. So, really, it was sort of a matter of just remembering the Ordinations, since they'd been there all along.

Things had begun—piece by piece—to make sense to her. Vessel Alpha remembered her mother, but Margo didn't. Margo had been a newborn when their mother died. Vessel Alpha remembered how soft her mother was. She remembered climbing into her mother's lap when she was tired. She remembered her mother swooping in and picking her up when she fell down. She remembered how her mother would kiss her boo-boos to make them better. And then one day her mother didn't wake up. Then, ever since that point, Vessel Alpha would be doing some regular everyday activity—playing ring-around-the-rosie in the schoolyard or unwrapping a jelly baby from its foil— and the feeling of her mother's soft body would come to her. And suddenly it would be like Vessel Alpha wasn't anywhere, just sort of swimming inside the picture of her mother. Vessel Alpha had always had trouble concentrating, and this was why: at any moment, this thing could happen. It always made her cry.

But now she understood. Mother Sunshine had explained to her. Her mother hadn't ever really existed. We all have the same mother, and the same mother is the same father—the Power. And the love that Susie had felt from her mother had actually been the Power. And even though her mother's vessel body had been discarded by the Power, the love was still there. It is always around us, everywhere, and it is beautiful.

And Vessel Alpha had begun to understand other things, too. Like, the reason she didn't do well in school school the way that Margo—no, Vessel Omega—Vessel Omega did, was that she, Vessel Alpha, was already a little closer to the Power.

Vessel Alpha felt tremendous relief when Mother Sunshine told her how it worked. The soft lap of her mother had been part of a material shell, just a vessel body. So, because her mother hadn't ever really existed, her mother hadn't ever really died. And also, Vessel Alpha would never have to go back to school, with its stupid times tables and fractions and county history lessons and mumblety-peg meets. She was part of something really important now. Because she was going to travel around with the Sunshine Family and find the *other* ordained ones, trapped in *their* temporary vessels but destined to build the pyramids on mountains all over. And then the next thing that was going to happen after that would be so wonderful, because the avalanches would come and everybody who helped out with the pyramid stuff would join the Twelve Hundred Celestial Angeldemons.

32

Margo had never hated before. She'd hear the word used, *hate*, and think it was useless, unimaginative. Even during the weeks when she would stare out the attic window at the dark mountain, certain that something was coming for her and her sister, she'd had no idea that this burning clamp of feeling was inside her, waiting to be awakened.

It's inside everyone.

33

Barbie had scopes. She had scopes and packs and night-vision goggles and a tight camo jumpsuit that unzipped to her navel and showed off the smooth crevice between her chest bumps. Ken had a matching jumpsuit, night-vision goggles, a canteen, and climbing lines. They both had ski masks. And they both had weapons: semiautomatic handguns with silencers.

Barbie also carried a bolo knife strapped to her arm.

They didn't talk much driving down the hill from the townhouse. It was dusk; the parrots were gathering in the palms. Barbie was behind the wheel; Ken leaned back in the passenger seat, looking up through the moonroof at the fluorescent birds.

Barbie turned right at the end of the driveway and wound down the curves of Floralinda Drive. In the fading glow of sunlight, the cactuses and aloes looked luminescent, and the sand scattered across the road twinkled.

At the place where Floralinda merged with Plane Boulevard, the place where the temperature abruptly dropped fifteen degrees and the succulents disappeared, Barbie pulled over behind a conical salt silo. There, in the backseat with the engine running, she and Ken fucked quickly and silently.

Afterwards, Barbie steered the car back onto Plane Boulevard's perfectly straight line. From there it would be the service road that skirted town.

Barbie had studied the maps of the mountain, which was enlaced by numerous dirt roads and trails. She knew that she and Ken might be embarking on a wild goose chase, but if Olga Schevschenko's information was correct, there was a good chance they'd at least find clues in the mountain, if not Margo and Susie Mouse.

It was now almost completely dark. The two-lane highway was punctuated only by telephone poles and small reflective markers. Ken reached over and rested his hand on Barbie's knee. She glanced over at him.

Things weren't supposed to change. Things were supposed to be the same every time, with every job—there would be slight variations, yes, in story and theme, but Barbie and Ken were not ever supposed to wind up somewhere different from where they started. This was the reason for Barbie's solemnity: she was starting to suspect that she had been wrong about this. She was starting to suspect that things could change, that this time *she* might be changed, and she could barely grasp what the implications would be. She'd never even thought about this stuff before.

It took an hour just to get to the service road, and another forty-five minutes of driving along its obtuse curve to get to their destination. A long stretch of the service road was a wasteland of strip malls, truck stops, and motels. They passed Paddy Skulldug's shop, a large bakery thrift store, a boxing gym. Then, for a while it became almost rural, with fields and the remainder of an old farm. The mountain loomed larger as they approached it.

Ken spread a map out on his lap and pointed his real mini-flashlight at it.

"It looks like we turn left at Foothill Road. There should be a little bridge over a creek."

"Right," said Barbie. "I think there's a parking lot for hikers there. We can leave the car and then walk over to the rangers' road on foot."

"What if we don't find them?" said Ken. "I mean, I'd never say this to H. or anything, but that is a possibility."

"We keep looking until we do," said Barbie.

"What if we do find them, but they're——"

"I don't know," said Barbie. She never said, *I don't know.*

"Okay," Ken said. "Gotcha." Barbie steered the car over the narrow bridge. They came to a gravel semicircle, where a wooden kiosk displayed information about the flora and fauna of the mountain. There they parked.

"We want to get as far away from the hiking trails as possible," said Barbie. "We'll focus on the fire trails instead."

"What kind of clues are we looking for?"

"Pyramids. Dodecahedrons. You know. Things like that."

34

It had been days since he'd heard from Barbie. Where was she? Sitting at the kitchen table with a tepid toddy and some gingersnaps before him, H. Mouse thought about going to the police—but he knew that it was too late. Waiting a week to report his daughters' disappearance would appear either psychotic or sociopathic, and definitely suspicious. He had tried out different approaches in his head, and none of them worked. He imagined himself calling his friend Bub Flytrap and saying, "Oh, you know, Bub, the oddest thing happened. I forgot to tell you, what with the election and all, but my daughters seem to have gone missing." Or confessing, "Bub, I have done something wrong: I hired Barbie and Ken." The thought of saying these things to Bub made his ears tremble.

The swearing-in ceremony was scheduled for the day after tomorrow. It would happen at three in the afternoon. The governor, television crews, the pageant queen, a marching band, and a middle-school choir would all be there. He was supposed to give a speech, and of course he hadn't even started writing one. Benjy Weevil was pulling together some bits from his past speeches and was going to stop by this afternoon to deliver them to H. Would Benjy notice that there were no youngsters in the house? H. doubted it. Benjy was too high-strung to be observant.

I would give up everything to get my daughters back, he said to himself, silently. But immediately he recognized that this wasn't true. If it were, he wouldn't be sitting here drinking whiskey at noon, waiting for mercenaries to call him with news. He crumpled even further down in his chair, his feet dangling over the floor, and his head practically resting on his diminished tummy.

He thought back to last week, the conversation he'd

with Barbie and Ken poolside. Barbie had asked if the taking of Margo and Susie might have been an act of revenge. He had said no, and he was still sure of that. But it had started to feel like some sort of punishment, something cosmic that was turning over the heavy stones of his conscience.

The real doorbell chimed its little chime. That would be Benjy Weevil; he was always five minutes early. H. Mouse told himself not to start thinking superstitious thoughts. Who knew where that would lead?

35

Father Sunshine had gathered the family around him.

"It's time to move," he said. "It's time to pack up and move on. The Power is saying it in the Old Language. The Power has ordained that we move south and west. We will start down the far side of the mountain when the hawks begin to prey this evening."

Margo's chest squeezed hard like a fist. She looked over at Susie, who was nodding and wearing that stupid, blank expression. Margo nodded too. Where was her father? She wanted to yell for him. She pictured him and tried to send him a message: We're alive, but they're taking us away.

The Sunshine family and Margo and Susie gathered in the kitchen nook. They all sat down before their plastic bowls of gruel and gray meat. Mother Sunshine whispered the blessing over the meal. Then everyone began to masticate.

"I'll gather the clothesline, the tin cans, the buckets," said Mother Sunshine, between bites.

"We'll cover over the latrine ditch," said Boy and Girl in unison.

"I'll patrol," said Father Sunshine. He pulled on some pants, stuck his pistol in his waistband, and slung his rifle over his shoulder.

36

Skipper sat in her room with all of the lights out. She had a hairbrush in one hand and a cordless microphone in the other. Barbie and Ken were both out on their mission. Skipper was used to being alone. She wasn't frightened to be alone, and she wasn't afraid of the dark. She knew the pathways of this townhouse by heart. When she was alone, she'd wander the halls and rooms, trailing one of her hands along the wallpaper, the plastic molding, the puffy furniture. Sometimes, she'd take off her jumper and blouse and lower herself into the lukewarm water of the pool. Tonight seemed like a good night to do that. She didn't understand how she made choices. Ideas would pop into her head, and she followed them. Why not?

She talked into the microphone, making her voice silky like Barbie's. "I feel like taking a swim," she said.

She walked in the dark to the elevator and took it to the first floor. Outside, it was warm and she could hear the parrots chattering in the driveway. She gazed out at the moonlit landscape. She tried to remember the first time she'd ever seen it, but nothing came to her. But she knew she had a past, because she remembered a different time. It had been a time when she'd believed she was in some kind of transitional phase and that she would soon become like Barbie. This had not happened. But surely the fact that she had memories meant that time was passing. And if that were true, didn't it mean she was always changing after all, along with everything else?

She pulled off the jumper and unbuttoned her blouse. She slid her baggy white underpants off. She was already barefoot. In the moonlight, she tipped her head forward on its neckball and looked down at her naked body. Her feet were flat. Not like Barbie's, which were extended in an arch. Skipper's hips were narrow. She pressed her hands to them, then moved her hands up, feeling the slight indentation of her waist. She pressed her chin to her chest. Her chestbumps were tiny. She stroked them, the way she'd seen Barbie stroking hers. She felt nothing, and she wondered what kind of feeling Barbie got from doing it.

She thought back to a couple of days earlier, when she had presented her armhole to Ken. She knew that to ask *why* was a departure from her nature; she understood that she was supposed to accept everything. But she wondered why Ken had rejected her that afternoon. At one point in time, in those earliest memories, she had assumed that when she finished her transition she would have her own kind of Ken; she'd assumed that someone would appear for her, someone who would take his head off his neck ball for her. But lately she had begun to suspect that there would be nobody.

She stepped into the pool. She heard a parrot in the distance. "Hello? Hello?" it called. "Come here," called another parrot. Skipper paddled to the middle of the pool and floated on her back. The sky looked like a ceiling. She tried again, reaching her cupped palm between her legs and rubbing with her thumb. She rubbed and rubbed. She tried making a noise like Barbie would make. "Ah, ah, ah," she said softly.

"Ah, ah, ah," said a parrot.

37

H. Mouse lay on his feather bed. The moon was low and bright, and its blue light flooded his room. He stared at the ceiling. The thing that flitted, day in and day out, around the very edge of his consciousness was beating its wings, trying to escape.

Right now, he was too weak. He let it out.

He remembered meeting her. He tried not to think about the scent of her, but it was as if he could smell it here, right now.

A new garage had opened out on the service road. As village councillor running for his second term, H. had thought it wise to get to know all of his constituents. And he'd given a speech at the beauty parlor about the importance of small businesses. He could still remember his favorite line from it: "The faith you have in your community counts in ways that go far beyond economics, my friends: it is the beating heart of the peace and prosperity we of this village benefit from each and every day. So, on behalf of all your fellow citizens, I say thank you."

He'd heard the owner of this shop had moved all the way from the far coast. So he'd driven out there to introduce himself and have his real rubber tires rotated. He'd parked his car outside the small, two-bay garage, and entered through the green painted door with the welcome sign. And there she had been. She was a little older than H. She had beautiful, dainty ears, he'd noticed right away, and a sweet, youthful voice. She'd said, "my son," not "our son," when she talked about the young mechanic. She'd said, "Petey's just tying up some loose ends out on the coast," and H. had assumed that Petey was her brother or cousin or plain old business partner. Later, in a hotel room two counties away, they would argue about this conversation. "I told you I was married," she'd cried. H. had held her and explained—again—"I thought that Petey was your brother," and she had snorted and pushed him away, repeating, "My *brother*?"

His heart pounded now, as he watched these pictures like transparent cartoons projected on the ceiling. That couldn't have been *him*; he remembered feeling as if some perverse being had taken over and was moving him around and speaking for him, making things up as it went along, having him do and say things he never would have dreamed he was capable of.

She'd also said it was as if some force from outside them had brought them together. But she seemed to like that idea that she had no control. She told him so, there in the heat of the garage on a quilt made of little patches all sewn together late one night. She was going to tell Petey. She had to. She wanted to be with H. She didn't want to sneak around. The guilt was going to kill her. "Look at me," she'd said, stretching out before him, luminous under the bulb of a real electric clip-on utility lamp. "Do you see how skinny I'm getting? I can't eat, I can't sleep."

From there, it got worse, but at the same time that he tried to break things off with her, he couldn't stay away from her. She would threaten to tell Petey; he would drive somewhere to talk her out of it. And then they'd be alone together. And so on. And so on. He groaned, alone now, thinking of the swirl of that time. How had he campaigned through all of it? Of course, his daughters had had no idea what was wrong with him. Margo, especially, had been worried. She kept telling him he looked sick and touching his forehead to see if he had a fever. Susie had become sullen; a concerned note had come from her teacher.

There had been the terrible final scene at her garage, when she said that if he wouldn't have her, she wouldn't just tell Petey, she would call the *State Eagle*. As soon as she'd mentioned the newspaper, he'd gone completely cold. He practically started to shiver. He lied through his teeth and told her everything was going to be okay. And then he had gotten in his car and driven, before dawn, directly from her garage to Floralinda. To Barbie and Ken. He didn't know the details of what Barbie and Ken had done after that, but he knew this much: it had involved every last drop of his savings and some pretty serious threats. The garage shut down that very day. In the afternoon, trembling with exhaustion and frayed nerves, he'd driven by in a car he'd borrowed from the Department of Lanes and Flowers. The place looked as if it had been closed for a decade.

Now he slid off his bed and went to the window. He looked out at the moonlight, at the dark mountains silhouetted there.

FIVE

38

For two days they had been combing the forest, circling the mountain, beating their way through brush, climbing over old stone walls, wading through marshes full of rotting leaves. Their scopes had been of no use. They had rested at night, wedged into one sleeping bag. Occasionally they would pause and unzip their jumpsuits, and one would quietly introduce an arm or foot into some hole of the other's.

On this, their third morning, Barbie and Ken were sitting next to each other on the trunk of a tree that had been snapped from its roots by lightning. At the jagged, severed base it was charred and hollowed out.

"I have an idea," said Ken.

"You do?"

"Tomorrow is his swearing-in, right?"

Barbie nodded.

"Well, if we don't find them today, we go back to Corporal Joe and buy two new ones for H."

Barbie looked sideways at Ken. Usually, when he was

idiotic it made her want to hump him. But now she just lowered her chin onto her lovely hands and said nothing.

"No?" said Ken.

"No," said Barbie. A picture of Skipper came into her head at that moment, and Barbie was overcome by a sudden, unfamiliar flash of worry. She'd never imagined before what it would be like to return to the townhouse one day and find that Skipper had disappeared. They couldn't just get a new Skipper if they lost this one. Barbie shuddered.

After a moment, she stood up and patted Ken on the shoulder. "Come on."

They tromped through a clearing full of brambles, and then came to a ditch. On the other side, they found themselves standing next to a shed beside one of the old fire trails. The shed's door hung on a single hinge. Barbie peeked inside. A rusty all-terrain vehicle sat there, covered in dead leaves.

"We could hot-wire it." Ken nodded at the vehicle.

"Too noisy," said Barbie. "But let's try this trail anyway."

They'd been hiking along the fire trail for just a few minutes when Barbie noticed something glittering on top of the dirt. Actually, it was a bunch of glittering things: chunks of mica arranged in some kind of shape.

"Wait," said Barbie. She bent her flexible legs and kneeled. "Does this look like a dodecahedron to you?"

Ken pulled Olga Schevshenko's envelope from Barbie's backpack. He held a piece of paper up next to the mica shape. "Yes," he said. "It really looks like a dodecahedron."

"Okay," said Barbie. "Now we're cooking. I say this is our trail."

They began to climb the steep incline of the dirt trail. Now and then, Barbie saw the faintest remnant of a tire track. As Barbie and Ken ascended, the air became thinner and colder. Crows cawed in the trees.

Then Barbie heard something that was neither a bird nor rustling leaves. It was the sound of metal clanking against metal. It was coming from off to the right of the trail. Barbie saw that someone had bushwhacked through the woods there and then covered up behind themselves with brambles and branches. The tire tracks were easier to see there in the muddy earth. "We've found something," said Barbie, pointing.

Barbie and Ken both patted their weapons. Then they stealthily left the fire trail and started along the new path.

It wasn't long before they saw it: a green van with a little chimney on its roof. A line was strung between two trees; that's where the noise had been coming from, a bunch of tin cans strung up on the line. They stood very still, watching.

And then he stepped out of nowhere: a small figure with a rigid gait, who began to march slowly around the van. He had a rifle strapped around his bare beige chest. His face was blank. After a couple of circles, he lifted something that was hanging around his neck. What was it?

Binoculars.

Barbie and Ken slipped behind trees.

The figure seemed to scan the woods. Barbie was pretty sure he hadn't seen them.

Then he began to circle again.

Two other, smaller, figures emerged. They were also stiff, and they were carrying a shovel.

"I think this is it," whispered Barbie.

"According to plan?" said Ken.

"According to plan," said Barbie.

39

Margo heard something, an uneven rustle or a crackle in the woods, a different kind of noise than the inflexible legs of the Sunshine Family would make. She looked around the van. She and Susie were the only ones inside. She climbed up onto one of the benches and looked out a window. She saw a flash of something pass between two trees. And then again, another flash, darting to a nearer tree. Her heart began to pound.

Susie must have heard it too, because suddenly she was up on the bench with Margo.

"What is it?" said Susie.

"I don't know," said Margo. But she did know. She *knew*. They were going to be saved.

"Oh no," said Susie. "Vessel Alpha, are they coming to get us?"

"I don't know what you're talking about," said Margo.

Susie sank down on the bench and closed her eyes. "It's okay," she said. "The Power will fell them."

Margo sat next to her and gave her a squeeze. For the first time in a while, she felt a little sorry for Susie. "Well, Vessel Omega, we'll see what the Power has ordained. You know it can be mysterious in its plans."

40

Before Father Sunshine knew what was happening, the intruders had him down on the ground. First they held his nose, and when his mouth opened, they stuffed something rubbery inside it. One of them had pulled his rifle off of him, and the other snapped a chain around his arms—which weren't meant to bend that way. Then the first one tied up his feet. He flopped on the dirt as they dragged him into the woods.

41

"Why don't you go and practice the ordinations. I'll keep a lookout," said Margo.

Susie nodded and hopped off the bench. She knelt on the mat in the corner and started to mutter, doing her best to sound like Mother Sunshine.

Margo peered out the window again just in time to see two tall, slim figures in camouflage jumpsuits jump on Father Sunshine like spiders on a fly. Tears of relief welled in her eyes as she watched him being dragged off into the woods. She looked right and left. From the right came Boy Sunshine and Girl Sunshine. They were carrying a shovel. They swiveled their heads a few times. Then they began to scream.

42

Barbie leaped toward the stunted-looking beings. They were loud. Ken followed her. Barbie grabbed the female and Ken grabbed the male. The female smelled weird, like sickness, like emptiness. Barbie and Ken held their handguns up to their captives' heads.

"Shut up," whispered Barbie hoarsely. "Shut up."

"It doesn't matter if you shoot us," said the male.

"All you'll kill is our flesh. These vessel bodies are rotting already anyway," said the female.

Barbie remembered what Olga had said about believers.

"Where are the others?" said Barbie.

"The others?" said the two in unison.

"Margo and Susie," said Ken.

"We don't know Margo and Susie," the two said.

Then Barbie saw something out of the corner of her eye. It was too fast for her. Before she knew what was happening, there was a horrendous bang, and Ken went down. Next to the van stood a figure she hadn't seen before, with frizzy yellow hair, huge round eyes, and a long dress. It held a gun.

Barbie glanced down at Ken and saw that a chunk of his neck was gone. She wanted to sink down next to him, but she couldn't. The male had run away, into the woods, but she still had to keep a grip on the female.

"Don't you dare shoot again," shouted Barbie. "I'll kill your daughter."

"She's nobody's daughter," said the shooter in the dress. "Nobody is anybody's daughter. We're Spirit Carriers for the Power. And you are dirt."

"All I want is the others," said Barbie. "And I'll leave you alone."

"Extinguish all of us," said the other. "We will join

the Celestial Angeldemons. And the Power will take its revenge on you."

Barbie moved the gun so that it was pressed against the head of her captive.

"So you won't mind when I blow this kid's brains out?" Barbie expected the female to struggle. Or beg her mother to comply. Or at least flinch. But she stood there, utterly still.

The yellow-haired one didn't move, either. She also stood utterly still, gun pointed at Barbie.

Then, out of nowhere, propelled by some ferocious burst of energy, appeared a tiny being in a dirty white dress.

43

Margo Mouse ran as fast as she could at Mother Sunshine, wielding Mother's rolling pin. She aimed for the lower half of Mother's rigid legs. Girl Sunshine saw Margo, but made no warning signals to Mother. At high velocity, Margo slammed into Mother Sunshine, who came down hard—but not without firing a shot at the blonde in the jumpsuit. Margo had Mother Sunshine on the ground. She jumped onto Mother's hard chest and started clobbering her head with the rolling pin. Margo didn't know she could make the noises she was making. She was yelling and crying and choking all at once. Mother Sunshine looked up at Margo, never breaking eye contact even as her head was pummeled this way and that.

Then Margo felt someone pulling at her, grabbing at the rolling pin. It was Susie.

Margo let go of the weapon. Susie took it from her. The two of them stood there, facing each other.

Then Margo looked over at their rescuer, who still gripped Girl Sunshine. Though she had lowered her gun.

"Who are you?" asked Margo.

"I'm Barbie."

"Did our dad send you?"

"Yes, he did."

"I told you he would save us," said Margo.

"Oh, Alpha, you're still attached to temporary, worldly things," said Susie.

Margo watched Susie lay the rolling pin down on the dirt next to Mother Sunshine's head. Then Susie turned and walked back to the van. Margo heard the sliding door open and shut.

The tin cans rattled.

"I'm Margo. Are you hurt?" Margo asked Barbie.

"She just got my hair," said Barbie. "But Ken's in bad shape."

44

It wasn't often that Barbie was stumped. In fact, had she ever before been stumped or flummoxed or paralyzed? No, she had not.

Pretty much every problem she and Ken had run into before had been solved, ultimately, by a combination of blackmail, a briefcase full of cash, and weaponry. But these nut jobs didn't care if they got H. Mouse's cash, and they didn't mind being hurt or even dying. They had no reputations to ruin. The male kid freak was off in the woods somewhere, the father was tied up but alive, and the mother was alive but battered. The female kid was right here in Barbie's grip, not resisting at all, standing as still as a statue. And Margo Mouse was standing there, dazed in the aftermath of her own violence, waiting for Barbie to save her from this sylvan hell.

Barbie felt a touch on her dainty ankle. It was Ken. He had managed to reach over to her. She looked down at him. There was a C-shaped divot in his neck. His head was covered in mud, and rotten leaves stuck to his dark hair. He stroked her heel a little.

"Ken," she said. "What the fuck do we do now?"

He coughed. She winced. "Your backpack," he said.

"What about my backpack?"

"Olga's papers," he whispered.

Barbie shimmied her backpack off her shoulders by unclipping its straps with her free hand. It dropped on the ground next to Ken. He wiggled himself around and managed to prop himself up enough to pull out the folder. After a few moments, he whispered, "Tell them the Power praises them for passing its test."

Barbie called out, as loud as she could, so the male back in the woods would hear, "The Power praises you for passing its test!"

"The first phase Ordination fulfillment has been completed. The foundation has been laid. The loyalty has been proven," Ken said.

"The first phase of Ordination fulfillment has been completed! The foundation has been laid! Loyalty has been proven!"

The female that Barbie was still clutching finally moved. She turned and looked at Barbie.

"The Power has ordained that your pyramidal tracts have reached the ultimate level of purity," Ken continued.

"The Power has ordained that your pyramidal tracts have reached the ultimate level of purity!"

Out of the woods appeared the young male one. He approached his sister. He wore a taut, blank grin.

Margo Mouse watched.

The young male stood next to the female and addressed Barbie: "So this is the test that the hieroglyphics prophesy?"

"Oh, yes," said Barbie.

Ken coughed and then addressed them directly: *"And the morn will come when the Power does test its faithful. And its faithful will offer up their husks as sacrifice. And a transfer shall unfold."*

"The transfer?" said the female.

"We give you the Spirit Carriers in exchange for . . . ?" said the male.

Barbie looked down at Ken, who glanced down at the papers.

"In exchange for a portal to the next level of purity," he answered.

The yellow-haired one on the ground lifted her bruised face. Barbie saw that she was shaking her head and trying to speak—but couldn't get any words out.

"If you release me," the female said, "I will fetch Vessel Omega."

Barbie looked at Ken again. He gave a painful little nod.

She let go. The two walked stiffly over to the van and disappeared behind it.

Margo Mouse ran over to Barbie and hugged her. And then she knelt down and touched Ken's face.

A few minutes later, the brother and sister returned with Susie Mouse between them.

"Go," said the male.

"You're sure?" asked Susie.

"Yes," said the female.

"You don't need me anymore?" said Susie. They shook their heads, and Susie began to weep.

45

Barbie and Margo and Susie managed to carry Ken to the fire trail. There, Margo and Susie waited with Ken while Barbie started down the mountainside. An hour later, they heard a rumbling motor. Then Barbie appeared, and they all went down the mountain on a kind of car with giant, bumpy tires. It was rusty and smelled like mildew.

Margo didn't want to ask Barbie and Ken how they knew her dad or why they had agreed to rescue her and her sister. She didn't want to think about where Barbie and Ken had gotten their guns. She didn't want to think about why the police hadn't come for them instead. She would push those thoughts into the obscure cupboards of her mind. Over the years they would sneak out now and then, though, in altered forms: she would have panic attacks during routine tasks; she would suffer bouts of insomnia; she would find herself doubting those closest to her and demanding reassurance; she would perform an act of great cruelty toward her father in spite of her fierce love for him. She would let him down. He would understand why.

Over the years, once in a while, Margo and Susie would get a little drunk and talk about what had happened. Susie would revise the story in her head and never admit how easily she had given herself to the Sunshine Family. Margo's contempt for her sister would never disappear—it would underlie every interaction they shared. One day, Margo would find herself sitting on a silk tuffet, watching Susie try on wedding dresses. Margo would tell herself to be happy because her sister was happy, but even then Margo would foster and guard the cold stone of distrust in her own heart.

Later yet, Margo would sit down with a pen and notebook and begin to write down what happened. She would get no farther than two sentences. Those sentences would disgust her, and although she would tell herself that it would be good for her to put it all into words, doing so would feel less like a cleansing act than an admission of guilt. Even though she'd know she had done nothing wrong, had in fact *been wronged*, writing about it would make her feel ashamed.

But none of that had happened yet. As she bounced over the rutted trail in the backseat next to Susie, Margo kept telling herself, "I'm safe now. I am safe. I am safe."

46

Before loading him into the ATV, Barbie had temporarily filled the hole in Ken's neck with some tree sap and tape—just to keep it from snapping. When they got back to the townhouse, it would have to be cleaned out and properly repaired by a professional. Barbie knew, deep down, that this injury would mean Ken's neck would always be delicate. She knew he'd never fully recover, that he'd have to be careful forever after, and that he'd probably always have to keep his neckball firmly inside his head. Even in a life such as Barbie's, sometimes things changed for good.

SIX

47

H. Mouse sat on the stage of the Justice Building auditorium next to the other officials who were about to be sworn in. The governor was giving a speech. Who knew what he was saying. H. Mouse's suit hung loosely on his depleted frame. He absentmindedly touched the gold pocket-watch inside his vest pocket. It had been a gift from the old State Judge, who had in turn received it from his predecessor. It was the sort of watch you have to wind. He could feel its rhythmic ticking.

He squinted past the bright lights to look at those in attendance. In the front, over on the right side of the aisle, were some members of the press. He could see the outline of Liz Fox, who was sporting a saucy cap and fur jacket. In the center, there were his new colleagues. And Benjy Weevil, who had changed his clip-on tie for the occasion.

In the middle of the room sat Margo and Susie. Margo had told him they were grown now and didn't need a chaperone. They could sit and manage fine all alone, she'd said. H. Mouse squinted and leaned forward. Susie was all dressed up, of course, in a pink dress—and she kept twisting around to look at all the others in the raked seats. Margo leaned forward. She did not crack a smile. She must have noticed her father looking at her, because she looked right back at him. She met his eyes and held the gaze.

H. Mouse heard the governor say his name. Applause erupted in the auditorium. He'd almost forgotten how popular he was.

He arose and approached the center of the stage, where the governor was waiting for him with the Big Book of Laws. Pressing down on the book, H. Mouse repeated each line of the oath of office. He found himself unable to make eye contact with the governor, though he forced himself by the end. As he completed the oath, the applause began once more, and the governor stepped to the side, making room for H. Mouse.

The speech he'd patched together with Benjy was waiting for him on the shelf under the podium. He smiled and nodded at the crowd and then made a motion for them to quiet down. He did his best to push his features into the pleased-yet-modest, verging-on-bashful expression he had perfected during his campaign.

He leaned into the microphone.

"My friends," he said. "Thank you."

His voice sounded strange to him, amplified and shooting out of the overhead speakers. There was a little more applause, and he hushed them again.

"Now, we are not here to celebrate. This is a ceremony of great solemnity, and much work lies ahead of us. I am looking forward to sitting down at my desk this very afternoon.

"But I did want to thank you, my friends. I was elected because the majority of our citizens believe what I believe. And they trust in me to make decisions based on these principles . . ."

He paused and took a deep breath. He felt dizzy under the lights.

". . . not politics or expedience. Our citizens believe that we are all essentially the same. They believe that we are, each of us, born in a state of grace and innocence. And they believe that no matter what someone may do, even if it causes great harm, it is the result of stresses and abuses that tainted their basic, innate moral sense."

Benjy had done a good job gluing together past speeches to make a new one. But as H. Mouse spoke these words, questions began to push their way into his mind: If what he was saying were true, then when did the relay of stress and abuse begin? Could ugly behavior be traced all the way back to the beginning of time? Or at least to the beginning of behavior itself?

"The role of the justice system is not to mindlessly punish. Rather it is to instruct and nurture. True justice, properly administered, acts as the good parent of society: disciplining its children with a firm yet caring, approach. So the children may take what they have learned and pass it on to the next generation."

His disembodied voice echoed through the room at a slight delay.

He might never really know what happened in the

green van up on the mountain. He might never really want to know. Margo and Susie had just been returned to him the night before. When they arrived, they were thin and dirty and dazed. Margo clung to Barbie; she didn't want to let go of her hand. Susie cried for hours. Neither of them said much about what they had been through. It was as if their brains couldn't yet encompass the experience, couldn't make it small enough. Barbie had been distracted. When H. made to get the balance of the cash he owed her and Ken, she said she'd rather he bring it to them some other time. She had to get Ken back to the townhouse right away. She had to make sure Skipper was okay.

"As your State Judge, I will make sure that those who commit acts of wrongness are punished. But they will be punished in a productive way. A cleansing way. A way we can, as a society, celebrate!" He let his voice rise over these final three sentences. "Thank you again, citizens!"

He was done. Sweaty and spent, he stepped away from the podium and made his way back to his chair. The governor approached the podium again to call on the next official.

Another speech began, and even as H. Mouse half-listened to it, compared it to his own, and decided his delivery was superior, his eyes came to rest on the two small figures of his daughters again. Margo was no longer looking at him; she seemed to be playing with something in her lap, maybe a tiny doll or a marble in the folds of her skirt. They are still so young, H. thought, and for a second, as if lit up by a flashbulb inside his mind, he saw the gray fur of their mother's pregnant belly; he remembered touching it, the taut skin. And then H. knew that someday—not now, not even soon—he would need to apologize to his daughters. It wouldn't matter whether they understood or granted forgiveness. It was clear to him: if he did not do it, he would die leaving a jagged scar behind, haunting Margo and Susie forever.

48

Skipper watched them from her bedroom window. They were all she had.

Ken was sitting on a clear inflatable deck chair, a white bandage wrapped around his patched neck.

Barbie floated in the blue water on her back. Her eyes were wide open. Her eyes were always wide open.